Oh Boy, No Boys!

"You don't think I can do it?"

"Well..."

Without thinking, I challenged, "Want to bet?"

Cassidy just looked at me.

Now that I'd said it, I liked the idea. It would be exciting ... fun. "I, Susanna Siegelbaum, hereby bet that I can last until June twenty-first without going out with a boy ... kissing a boy ... or even flirting with a boy."

Other Point paperbacks
you will enjoy:

Something's Rotten in the State of Maryland
by Laura A. Sonnenmark

A Royal Pain
by Ellen Conford

Dear Lovey Hart, I Am Desperate
by Ellen Conford

If This Is Love, I'll Take Spaghetti
by Ellen Conford

SUSANNA SIEGELBAUM GIVES UP GUYS

JUNE FOLEY

SCHOLASTIC INC.
New York Toronto London Auckland Sydney

ISBN 0-590-43700-3

12 11 10 9 8 7 6 5 4 3 2   3 4 5 6 7/9

Printed in the U.S.A.   01

To: Hedy Straus, my first friend.
To: Sheila Sweeney Fortune and
Jacqueline Thomas Cerenzo, without whom I never
would have lived through high school.
And to: Max Lindenman and Bobby Stark,
two fans of both the Mets and Melville.

SUSANNA SIEGELBAUM GIVES UP GUYS

One

"Heathcliff!" I yelled. "Heeeeeeeeeeeeeeeathcliiiiii-iiiiif!"

"Siegelbaum, *shh*," whispered my best friend, Annie Cassidy.

"You know I always get this way on the first day of spring," I reminded her.

"Even though it feels like winter?" As an icy gust swept by, Cassidy scrunched up her shoulders under her parka.

"Especially when it's windy," I said, throwing my head back. "I feel like I'm on the moors, searching for my beloved, like Catherine looking for Heathcliff in *Wuthering Heights*." I called again: "Heeeeeeeeeeeeeath-cliiiiiiiiiiif!"

"Siegelbaum, please, we're on State Street, I'm holding a box of pizza, and people are looking at us."

"They are? Terrific!" Across the street, I spotted

1

Lance Levine, an old boyfriend. "One of the people looking at us could turn out to be my beloved." I waved and called out, "Hey, Lance!" and he smiled and yelled, "Hey, Susanna!" before walking on.

As Cassidy and I walked past Central High, some teenage boys were playing a pickup basketball game. Naturally, I checked them out. But basketball was boring unless boys were wearing those cute short uniforms. Then I realized something. "Cassidy, I've gone out with one of those entire teams."

"One by one, of course," she said.

It was true. I'd gone out with Todd Lane, Junior Jackson, Paul Hoffman, and the brothers Brian and Brendan Seely. Just once or twice each — movies or parties or hanging out at the mall — but still. "Maybe I could get into *The Guinness Book of World Records*."

"Sometimes I wonder about you," Cassidy said.

"What's left to wonder? You know me better than you know your sisters. We've been best friends for nine years — since we were six."

"And you've had boyfriends almost since then."

"Before. In nursery school Charles Milton slipped me a handful of Cheerios, I put one on my finger, and told him we were married."

For some reason, Cassidy looked sad. I had to cheer her up. "Okay, you haven't had your first date yet, but it's not like you have a hump," I said.

I could tell she didn't quite get my point, because her eyebrows suddenly came together. They didn't have too far to go, either, since her mother wouldn't let her pluck them. "I mean, in my opinion you're a great human being, plus you look like a model, even in your Sacred Heart uniform."

"Which was designed to make every girl look like

2

a combination of a nun and a Marine," she said. "Thanks, Siegelbaum." From her five feet, eight inches, she smiled down at my five feet.

"Your one and only problem, Cassidy, which I've told you a zillion times, is that you're insanely shy around boys."

"And I wasted my first semester of high school having that silly crush on my English teacher."

"Mr. Angelucci was definitely a mistake. But on the other hand, you've been getting along fantastically well with Slop-Spelled-Backwards." Robby Pols was the editor of *The Voice*, Sacred Heart's newspaper, which Cassidy worked on as a reporter. He'd asked her to their school's Winter Dance, but because of her weird thing for Mr. Angelucci, she'd turned him down. Then she was sorry. "I'll bet one of these days you get the guts to call Robby and ask him out."

"I did call him."

My head snapped around and up. "You did?"

"But when he answered the phone, I hung up."

"Oh, no." I was about to put my arm around Cassidy to comfort her, when I saw a teenage boy coming toward us. "Hey, how're you doing?" I asked with a giant smile.

Laughing, he said, "Real good," as he walked by.

"Who was that?" whispered Cassidy.

"Branwell Brontë," I said.

"Branwell Brontë?"

"I don't know who he is. I never saw him before. But doesn't he look like he should be named Branwell Brontë?"

"Wasn't that the name of Emily and Charlotte Brontë's brother?"

"Oh, yeah. For a minute, I really thought I'd made

it up." Of course, Cassidy knew that Emily Brontë wrote my favorite novel, *Wuthering Heights,* and Charlotte Brontë wrote another great one, *Jane Eyre,* and their other sister, Anne, wrote a couple of novels, too. That was the main thing Cassidy and I had in common: We both loved books. In fact, next to boys and Cassidy and my family, I liked books better than anything. "But can't you just imagine someone with the romantic name of Branwell Brontë writing a love poem about me?" I asked.

"Do very many words rhyme with Siegelbaum?" she replied.

"He could always rhyme Susanna."

"With banana."

Grabbing Cassidy's arm, I said, "I have a terrific idea! Someday I'll write a TV series about the family life of Charlotte, Emily, Anne, and Branwell Brontë. And guess what I'll call it?"

"What?"

"The Brontë Bunch."

Arriving at my house just then, we were both laughing — the perfect start for a sleepover.

My parents were at a party, so we had the place to ourselves, but we still headed for my attic room. It was chaos. I loved it. And Cassidy preferred it to the way her mother made her and her sisters keep their rooms — so neat and clean the only thing you could do in them was sleep or perform surgery.

Although cold winds were howling outside, Cassidy and I were warm and cozy, sitting cross-legged on the bed eating pizza.

"I'll help you tell Robby Pols how you feel about him," I told her. "I'll go up to him and sing that Beatles song, 'She loves you, yeah yeah yeah.' "

"No no no!" Cassidy said, her voice a squeak.

"Okay, okay. But Cassidy, you've got to ask Robby out. He'll say yes, I'm absolutely positively sure. I just know he likes you soooooooooo much." I licked tomato sauce from my fingers.

Cassidy was still nibbling on her first plain slice when I picked up my third, with peppers, onions, sausage, and anchovies, and began gobbling it. Suddenly she raised her chin and got a determined expression on her face. "I'm going to ask Robby out."

"Hooray!" I almost clapped my left hand into what remained of the pizza I was holding in my right.

After a two-second smile, Cassidy bit her lip. "What should I ask him to do? Go to the movies?"

"Forget it. You like love stories, and Robby's favorite movie is probably *Attack of the Killer Tomatoes*. Besides, that's too ordinary for your very first date. You should do something special."

She turned paler than ever.

"But maybe with other people around, in case you go into shock."

She stared at the ceiling for a minute. "The Latin Club banquet?"

"Perfect! I'll be there with you!" Not many kids were crazy enough to take Latin, so Sacred Heart had to team up with my private school, The Willow School, for the banquet.

"It would be really nice to have you there for moral support," Cassidy said. "Who are you asking?"

"I've got it narrowed down to Jeremy Walker, Shawn Rountree, or Richard Trehuba," I said, plucking an anchovy from the pizza and popping it into my mouth. "What are you wearing? I already made my toga, but it's sort of tight around the tush."

5

"I made mine, too. It's what my mother calls a 'floral print.' I know they didn't have them in ancient Rome, but my mother only buys sheets with flowers." Cassidy's lip got more teethmarks. "Siegelbaum, I'm going to call Robby right now."

"Do it." I handed her the phone. She picked up the receiver, pushed the buttons, and held the phone to her ear. Watching her, I realized she'd memorized the number. I pantomimed praying.

All of a sudden she looked like she'd been struck by lightning. "Robby, hi, it's . . ." She stared at me.

"Annie Cassidy," I reminded her.

"It's Annie Cassidy . . . um . . . and I . . . I was just wondering . . . since I take Latin and you take Latin and . . ." She hesitated again.

I whispered, "Carpe diem," Latin for "seize the day" — in other words, hurry up and do it while you can.

"Um . . . will you go to the Latin Club banquet with me next Friday night?"

Grinning already, I thought, Now he's going to say yes. He's got to say yes. Say yes, Robby. Hurry up and say yes!

"Fine," she said, her voice high and thin. "Of course." Hanging up, she looked totally dazed.

"What'd he say? What'd he say? He said yes, right?"

Cassidy just nodded.

"Hooray!" I dropped my pizza on the bed and hugged her.

TWO

That week, Cassidy and I not only walked to school together and hung out after, we called each other every night and talked and talked. She had a hundred questions, and a thousand doubts. I answered all her questions and kept reassuring her about how terrific she was, how much Robby liked her, how much she liked him, how well they got along, how much fun he was, and how much fun it was, basically, to go out with just about any boy.

I finally asked Jeremy Walker to be my own date for the banquet. He was the one I figured would look best in a toga. Since he was on my school's basketball team, I'd had a chance to check out his bod. There'd been a time when I'd rated boys' buns, from F to A+, but recently I'd decided it was immature. Now I took into consideration other attributes — for example, shoulders, chest, and legs.

7

When Jeremy and I were walking to the banquet, I must have said hi to six or seven guys I'd gone out with.

"Ms. Popularity," Jeremy said, putting his arm around me proudly and maybe a little jealously.

I looked into his eyes, which were green, like mine. We looked really good together.

"Just like ancient Rome, right?" I said, as Jeremy and I stepped into The Willow School cafeteria, decorated for the banquet.

"More like DeLorenzo's Pizzeria," Jeremy said.

I called out to kids, telling them how terrific they looked. "But I guess the noblest Roman of them all was Ralph Lauren," I said. "His name's on so many togas."

"Check out Ben Green," Jeremy said. "He's wearing a Smurfs toga."

"How about Jessica Rockwell? Can you believe she's sewn an alligator onto her toga?" I groaned.

Then Cassidy and Robby came in. She looked gorgeous in her floral-print toga. And she and Robby looked great together. He was her height, with a strong build, sandy hair, glasses, and a really cute face.

"Salve!" I shouted, from across the room.

They came over and returned the Latin greeting. Cassidy flashed me a big smile that meant: I'm glad I decided to do this!

In seconds, Jeremy and Robby were talking about sports. Jeremy said, "I heard that Ben Green tapes the TV hockey games and then erases everything but the fights."

While Cassidy made a face, I said, "I have to get into the kitchen. Somehow I ended up on the serving committee. Vale for now, you guys. See you soon with porculus assus and mustum."

"You want to translate?" Jeremy asked.

"Roast suckling pig and supposedly wine, but really grape punch," I said.

I came out of the kitchen a few minutes later, balancing a tray filled with food. Service was not my middle name. I'd never done this before. And the first person I had to serve was Sister Annunciata, Sacred Heart's Latin teacher, who looked so old she was rumored to have dated Julius Caesar. Somehow I lost my grip on the tray, and several slices of pork slid onto Sister Annunciata's lap, then under the table.

"Oh, no. Oh, brother. Oh, Sister, I'm sorry. I mean, mea culpa, Soror." Sister seemed to be offering up a silent prayer.

Right after I served Sister again, I spotted Jeremy — talking to Jessica across the room, outside my serving area. I planned to stare at him until he looked at me. But he kept talking to her. I went back to serving, kidding around while I did it, and a few minutes later looked at Jeremy again. He and Jessica were laughing together. I began to flirt with all the boys near me.

When I finished serving, I sat at a table next to Cassidy, who was next to Robby. Kids from both Sacred Heart and The Willow School were there, too.

"Where's Jeremy?" Cassidy asked.

I pointed my thumb at Jessica. She and Jeremy were close together, whispering.

Cassidy just looked, her eyes getting bigger and bigger.

I nudged her. "It's no big deal," I said, and immediately turned to the boy next to me with a smile.

It happened to be Ben Green, who was wiping his mouth on the hem of his toga.

All the Latin students were now getting into the spirit of the Roman Empire — the decline of the Roman Empire. Even though the mustum was just punch, lots of kids acted drunk. Somebody covered the "Boys' Room" sign with a new one: "Vomitorium." Instead of trying to talk in Latin to the kids serving dessert, everybody was yelling, "Yo, slave!" Ben Green was blowing his nose on his toga. Then he turned to me and pointed at a button he was wearing that said, "Oscula Me, Ego Loquor Latinam" — Kiss Me, I Speak Latin. I turned away so fast I risked whiplash.

Cassidy and Robby were gazing into each other's eyes, and I was so glad. Quickly, I glanced at the next table. I saw Jessica and Jeremy also gazing into each other's eyes, and I wanted to pour mustum on their heads.

"Friends, Romans, classmates, lend me your ears," said Joe Attanasio, president of Sacred Heart's Latin Club, from the head table. "Come on down for the translation contest!"

"Sister Annunciata said I had to enter," Cassidy told me. "I'm so nervous. Will you come with me?"

Out of the corner of my eye, I watched Jeremy finally leaving Jessica's side and coming my way. "Sure, why not?" I said, standing up.

"Robby?" Cassidy asked.

"Goodus luckus," Robby said. "Both of yousus."

I put my all into winning that translation contest. I not only avoided looking at either Jeremy or Jessica, I didn't look at anybody at all until half an hour later, when I beat out Cassidy by being the first to translate "Omnia vincit amor" as "Love conquers all."

10

I saw Robby grinning at Cassidy, who blushed. Then I saw Jeremy back with Jessica. They were feeding grapes to each other. They look like a couple, I thought.

A flash, like a bolt of lightning, came into my head: *I've never been part of any boy-girl couple!* I suddenly realized that going out with lots of boys was like not going out with boys at all, in a way, because I'd never known a boy really well. I also realized that since Cassidy and Robby had worked together on their school newspaper for months, she already knew Robby better than I'd ever known a boy. Some mentor! Some expert!

Cassidy raised my hand over my head in a winner's pose while kids cheered. My heart was racing, my knees weak, and my face so hot it was probably the color of mustum. I managed to smile as I held up two fingers in a V for victory. But I was still basically out of it, or I never would've given that high five to Sister Annunciata.

Next thing I knew, Jeremy was coming up to me. "Susanna, I've been looking all over for you," he said.

I pictured him laid out on a platter with an apple in his mouth. "If only I knew how to say 'Bug off' in Latin," I said.

I walked away, my head high. I even smiled and waved back at Richard Trehuba and Sam Chu and Shawn Rountree. Then I walked out of the room and the building, toward home . . . alone.

Three

There was a full moon when I walked the few blocks to my house. I stared up at it while I walked. Then, under that full, white, brightly shining moon, I made a decision: I was going to give up guys. I'd tell Cassidy I was just going to rest from romance. But I couldn't lie to myself: I was really going to recuperate from the shock of finding out I'd never had a romance.

Suddenly the moon was hidden by a cloud. How dark and cold it seemed! I was glad to be close to home.

I threw my laurel wreath in the garbage.

My parents were laughing in the TV room. I stuck my head inside. "Hi, Elaine, hi, Jerry." For as long as I could remember, I'd called them by their first names. Elaine was a gynecologist at the University Women's Center, and Jerry painted at home two weekdays and was an art therapist at a hospital the other three.

12

Elaine, who was little and blonde, like me, was sitting on the sofa, her bare feet up on the coffee table. Jerry, medium-sized with crazy curls and green cat's-eyes I'd inherited, was lying on the sofa with his head on Elaine's lap. They were sharing a bowl of popcorn, which sat on Jerry's chest and shook as he laughed.

"How was the banquet?" Elaine asked.

Even though I was close to my parents, some things I didn't want to share with them. "Fabulous. Cassidy and Robby got along really well. Cassidy was runner-up in the translation contest, and guess who won? Your darling daughter."

They congratulated me. "Come watch this movie with us," Elaine said. "We've rented Charlie Chaplin's *Limelight*. It's wonderful."

"I'll even give you the honor of holding my feet," Jerry said, lifting up his feet so I could slide under.

Holding my nose, I said, "Thanks, anyway."

In my room, I grabbed the top cassette from my collection and put it on to play while I got into my flannel nightgown.

When would spring really come? I couldn't wait! I stared out the window, wishing for bright yellow buds on the forsythia bushes, instead of frost. As I got into bed, I realized that the song playing was Elvis's "Are You Lonesome Tonight?"

I couldn't help thinking of how Jeremy had dumped me. Even though I didn't know him very well, it hurt to be dumped by him. I flashed back to Jeremy and Jessica, laughing . . . whispering . . . feeding each other grapes. I thought of Robby grinning, and Cassidy blushing.

I reminded myself that I, Susanna Siegelbaum, was going to give up guys. I was going to take a break from

13

boys. Then I'd start over and everything would be all right. No big deal.

When I woke up the next morning, my first thought was: I'm giving up guys. I said it to myself over and over, to get used to it. I'm going to give up guys, I'm going to give up guys, I'm going to give up guys, I kept repeating. By the time I'd had breakfast, I was ready to tell Cassidy.

"I'm going to give up guys," I said softly to myself when I knocked on the door to her house.

"Hey, Susanna!" "Hi, Susanna!" "Susanna-Banana!" Cassidy's little sisters, also known to us as The Three Stooges, descended upon me as they let me in the house.

"Susanna, look!" Jane, an eleven-year-old jock, demonstrated a karate move by punching me in the stomach.

I got her in a wrestling hold, then released her.

"Where'd you learn that?" she asked.

"Bubby Bergman."

"Bubby Bergman? Is he a wrestler, like Hulk Hogan?"

"She's my grandmother — a wrestling fan."

"Listen, Susanna." Ten-year-old Lisa sat at the piano and played "The Minute Waltz" for what seemed like hours.

I applauded, then ran over and pounded out "Tutti Frutti."

"Did your grandma teach you that?" Lisa looked amazed.

"Susanna, say hi to my new pet," eight-year-old Chrissy interrupted. She shoved a tiny turtle so close I got cross-eyed.

14

"What happened to your old pet, Robby the frog?" He'd been named after *the* Robby, who'd been coming home with Cassidy to work on their school newspaper while she baby-sat.

"He croaked," Chrissy said.

"Naturally. He's a frog," I said.

"I mean he died." Tough Chrissy got tears in her eyes.

"I'm sorry," I said, putting my arm around her. "Your turtle's terrific, though."

Chrissy grinned. "Okay — I'm naming him Terrific Turtle, T.T. for short. I got him to practice being a vet. I just hope he gets sick so I can make him better."

"How do you know when a turtle's sick?" Jane asked. "Where are you gonna put the thermometer?" She cracked up.

Chrissy said, "Us vets know animals. So that includes you, you big fat pig."

"Mommy, Chrissy and Jane are fighting!" cried Lisa.

"And Lisa's tattling!" Chrissy screamed.

With a sigh, Cassidy emerged from the kitchen.

"Can we talk?" I said softly, and she quickly nodded. We dashed past her squabbling sisters, up the stairs, and into the only place where there was any privacy. Cassidy perched primly on the toilet seat. I stretched out in the tub.

"Siegelbaum, you disappeared from the banquet," she said.

Making myself grin, I said, "All I want to know is, did you have a great time or did you have a great time on your first date?"

"It was one of the best times of my life," she said. "Robby's just so nice. On the way to the banquet, he said he'd called me lots of times, but every time I answered he got scared and hung up."

"Hey, he was brave to say that."

"Wasn't he? So of course I said I'd done the same thing. And then . . . and then he asked me out for next Saturday night."

"Wow!" I sat up. Now I'd tell her *my* big news.

"Siegelbaum, I'll never forget how you helped me," Cassidy said. "It's because of you that I asked Robby out, and he asked me out. Now you and I can double-date. It'll be wonderful. We . . ." She laughed. "I didn't mean to interrupt. You were saying . . ."

"I was saying, I'm giving up guys."

She stared at me. "Pardon me?"

"I'm giving up guys."

"You?" Her eyes got very big. "Why?"

"I . . ." There was a pounding on the door. "Let us in. Mom says we have to brush our teeth," Jane said.

"I want to brush my hair," said Lisa.

Chrissy said, "And I've gotta do number one and number . . ."

Cassidy and I were out of there and in her room within seconds. We sank to the floor, our backs against the door, and she looked expectantly at me.

"I just want a rest from romance," I said. "I've gone out with soooooo many boys. I need a vacation."

"Really?" she squeaked.

"Uh-huh." To show her how casual I was, I yawned. When I opened my eyes, she was staring at me.

"For how long?" she asked.

I hadn't thought about that. "Mmm . . . until the end of school. June twenty-first . . . three months."

"Siegelbaum!"

"You don't think I can do it?"

"Well . . ."

Without thinking, I challenged, "Want to bet?"

Cassidy just looked at me.

Now that I'd said it, I liked the idea of a bet. It would be exciting . . . fun! "I, Susanna Siegelbaum, hereby bet that I can last until June twenty-first without going out with a boy . . . kissing a boy . . . or even flirting with a boy."

She looked very serious. "You'd have to be on your honor, since we go to different schools."

"I was a Girl Scout, remember?"

She laughed. "There's nothing to bet anyway. We hardly ever have any money."

"Okay, here's the deal," I said, thinking faster than I'd ever thought in my life. "If I win, you buy me a double-dip ice-cream cone, with sprinkles."

Cassidy said, "And if I win, do you buy me a double-dip . . . ?"

There was a knock on the door. Another. Another.

"If you win," I told Cassidy, "I take your place baby-sitting with your sisters one afternoon a week for a year."

"Let us in!" "It's not fair!" "Hurry up!"

Cassidy's eyes were enormous. "Siegelbaum, you can't be serious."

"I am. Come on, Cassidy. It'll help me give up guys, by making it a game. It'll be fun."

"We're going to break this door down!" "So, there!" "Yeah!"

"Please?" I said, softly and sweetly. "Pretty please with sprinkles on it?" I extended my hand.

"Siegelbaum . . ."

17

"Okay, you asked for it!" "Here we come!" "One . . . two . . ."

I grabbed Cassidy's hand and shook it. "It's a deal," I said, smiling. We both stood up.

Then Cassidy opened the door and Jane, Lisa, and Chrissy fell in.

Four

On Monday morning, as usual, Cassidy and I walked together to Sacred Heart, and after that I kept walking four blocks further to The Willow School. Lots of boys said hi to me as we got near Sacred Heart. I smiled and said hi back, but hardly anything more. "Notice how I'm not flirting with any boys," I told Cassidy.

Then Kevin Enchi, one of the cutest boys in my own school, yelled hi from across the street. I waved and smiled, and sighed deeply.

"Cassidy, I really don't know if I can give up boys for three months. It's already making me feel weird." I pretended to start to faint.

"Don't worry, I know first aid," Cassidy said, giggling as she tried to hold me up.

"No, no, let *him* resuscitate me."

Cassidy laughed so hard she let go of me, and I fell to the ground.

Inside my school, some kids congratulated me on winning the translation contest. "Gratias, gratias," I thanked them.

All of a sudden Jeremy and Jessica were in the hall, walking toward me. I'd ignore them, naturally. Better yet, I'd ignore them while sweeping past with a boy. I grabbed the arm of the nearest boy.

"Hey, Susie, baby. Can't even control your urges on school property, huh? I must be irresistible."

The boy was Ben Green. I made myself smile at him as we passed Jeremy and Jessica, but he was definitely the most resistible boy I'd ever met. Not only did he tape hockey games and erase everything but the fights, wear a Smurfs toga on which he wiped his mouth and nose, and try to get me to oscula him — sometimes in the halls at school he wore a plastic pig's snout.

Right now, at least, the only nose on his face was his own. Then I looked further up: An arrow seemed to be going through Ben's head. If only it really were! "See you," I said, releasing his arm and rushing into biology class.

Over the next few days, giving up boys wasn't much of a problem. It was kind of fun. Cassidy and I kept goofing about it. There was a tiny touch of softness and warmth in the air on Wednesday, and I persuaded Cassidy to celebrate spring with the first ice-cream cones of the season. At the soda fountain, she asked for her usual — vanilla. "What would you like, Siegelbaum?"

"Boys . . . enberry," I said.

The girl behind the counter said, "Jimmies?" That was what some people in our town called sprinkles.

"Yeah, please, jimmies," I said.

Cassidy whispered to me, "And also Joeys and Jeffreys and Johnnys."

After school on Thursday, we went to the library. "Maybe some new books will get my mind off boys," I said.

"Be careful. Remember when you went on that diet and decided to go to the library to get your mind off food?"

"Yeah. I was planning some heavy reading — *War and Peace . . . Crime and Punishment . . .* and *Hamlet.*"

"Except when you told me about it, you said, '*War and Peas . . . Crime and Peppermint . . .* and *Omelet.*' " Cassidy suddenly got dreamy-eyed. "That reminds me, Robby brings an enormous kielbasa sandwich for lunch almost every day."

"A kielbasa hero, huh? Hey, I guess you could say Robby's *your* kielbasa hero."

We were laughing as we walked into the library. That made me think of the first time Cassidy and I met — in the library children's room when we were six. We'd both reached for the same picture book at the same time. I got it. Although maybe she let me have it. Anyhow, I'd said, "Let's look at it together." It was a funny book, and I could still see us sharing it, Cassidy holding her hand over her mouth to cover her giggles, me guffawing so hard I fell over backward in my chair. We'd been sharing books and jokes and a whole lot more ever since.

Friday morning was even more springlike, and Cassidy and I more giggly than usual. Waiting for her after school that day, I saw the first forsythia buds. When she came, Robby was with her.

"Hey, the kielbasa hero," I said.

His face reddened, and then Cassidy's turned the same shade. But he quickly said, "What's up, Susanna? Get any new music?"

"I just got something from the fifties," I said. "Patti LaBelle and the Bluebelles, singing 'I Sold My Heart to the Junkman.' "

"Sounds real romantic," Robby said. Then he and Cassidy both got red again.

I started imitating Patti LaBelle, but Cassidy was looking at Robby instead of me. And Robby was looking at Cassidy. It was the first time in history that my Patti LaBelle imitation had gone unnoticed. I had to shriek out a tremendously high note to finally get their attention.

Cassidy, Robby, and I walked to Saint Aloysius Grammar School, picked up her sisters, and went on to the park. Instead of shooing the Stooges away, Robby talked and played with them. They behaved better around him — not human, but close. Robby got everybody playing Frisbee, trying cartwheels, picking wildflowers. A good time. Although maybe not quite as good as just Cassidy and me together.

Saturday morning, of course, Cassidy cleaned. She used to call her mother Our Lady of Good Housekeeping, because she was such a dedicated homemaker. Then when Cassidy was eleven, her father was killed in a car accident. It was so horrible. She still hardly talked about him, even though they'd been really close. After Mr. Cassidy died, Mrs. Cassidy went to work as a secretary. Now she was an office manager, and also studied accounting at night. And now the

Cassidy kids did the housework together, one morning a week. Meanwhile, I was playing my drums, backing up the Beatles on "A Hard Day's Night," Little Richard on "Good Golly, Miss Molly," and Elvis on "Blue Suede Shoes."

When Cassidy and I rode our bikes that afternoon, she talked a little more than usual, mostly about Robby. "I can't believe I have a Saturday-night date," she said. And I said, "I can't believe I don't." We both laughed, naturally, but somehow both our laughs sounded a little odd.

That night, I called my grandmother, my bubby, who'd moved to Florida this past winter. "How's your aerobics class?" I immediately asked.

"Darling, you're calling me on a Saturday night to ask about my aerobics class?" she said.

You could fool both of my parents some of the time, you could fool one of my parents most of the time, but you could never ever fool Bubby, not for a single second. That was one of the things I loved most about her . . . usually. My busy parents hadn't realized yet that I'd given up guys, which was great, because I didn't feel like discussing it with them. But I didn't want to discuss it with Bubby, either. Especially not with Bubby — although I didn't know why.

"I'm really curious about your class, Bubby," I said.

"If you don't want to tell me why you don't have a date, why don't you just tell me that you don't want to tell me?" Bubby said. While I sighed in reply, she said, "My class is going very nicely, considering that at my age, just getting out of bed in the morning is an aerobic exercise. And I'm getting to know another woman in the class — Mrs. Santini. After we exercise, we go out for pastries. She's teaching me to crochet, too, darling. Guess what I'm crocheting for you?"

"A doily?" Who even knew what a doily was? But it was definitely crocheted.

"A bikini," Bubby said.

"All riiiiiight!"

"And what's happening with you?"

"Uh . . . tell me more about Mrs. Santini."

She paused, then said, "Well, she's a widow, like me. Her first name is Betty. And you know that my first name is Beatrice, but I was called Beattie as a girl. So now we're Betty and Beattie."

"Sounds like the Bobbsey Twins," I said.

"Exactly. *The Bobbsey Twins Grow Up — and Grow Old.*"

Bubby didn't noodge me about not having a date, and when I said good-bye I was smiling.

On Sunday morning I picked up Cassidy for Mass. Mostly I went to be with her, but it was also interesting to check out another way of life. My family was Jewish, but not religious. I enjoyed Cassidy's church's stained-glass windows, incense, and what Cassidy called the vestments but I called the costumes. The kneeling, I could have done without.

"How was your date?" I asked, as soon as I saw Cassidy.

"Wonderful." She was beaming. "We went to the movies and for pizza after. The only part that wasn't wonderful was when Robby picked me up. Jane said, 'Are you going to kiss Annie good-night?' and Lisa said, 'It's only their second date!' and Chrissy said, 'What do you think Annie is — a slut?' "

"Oh, no."

24

"But Robby's so calm. He didn't seem to mind. He didn't even mind when my mother asked a million questions."

"She didn't ask for a urine sample, to test for drugs?"

Cassidy didn't seem to hear this. "Siegelbaum, he's so nice."

"So . . . *did* he kiss you good-night?"

She didn't say a word, just blushed.

"Hooray!" I cheered. "Is he a good kisser?"

When Cassidy looked at me, her expression changed so many times, so fast, I couldn't interpret a single look. Finally, she looked away, toward the McIlhenny's front yard. "Aren't the forsythia beautiful when they're in bloom?" she said.

Cassidy showed up Monday after school with Robby. Again, the three of us picked up the Stooges and again we had fun. But Robby also showed up Tuesday morning and afternoon, Wednesday morning and afternoon, and Thursday morning and afternoon.

There he was again on Friday morning! Now I was annoyed. And so was Cassidy, I could tell. Several times I saw her frowning.

As she and Robby were about to turn off toward their school, she said, "Siegelbaum, after school today Robby and I are working on the *Voice* at my house."

"I'll help," I said.

"Nah, don't bother," said Robby. "It's no fun for you."

"It's really boring," Cassidy said.

Aha — her way of telling me she'd much rather hang out with me than slave on the school paper and see Robby for the fifth day in a row!

I went right home after school and as soon as I

figured Cassidy would be home, I called her. "Hi, it's me. Listen, I know you've been wanting to talk about Robby."

"Siegelbaum, you're so smart."

"I know what you're going through. But all you have to do is tell the truth."

"Really?" Her voice was small.

"Sure. Just say it. Say, 'I like you a lot, but we're spending too much time together. I really hope you'll understand.' "

"Oh, I couldn't say that," she said.

"You can so. Stand up for yourself. You've got a right to be with whoever you want."

"I know, but . . ."

"And if you have to hurt somebody's feelings, it's too bad, but hey, that happens sometimes. That's life."

Silence.

"Come on, Cassidy, you can do it."

I heard a sigh. Then Cassidy said, "Siegelbaum, you know how much I like you, but we're spending too much time together. I'd like to be alone with Robby more. At school, we're always surrounded by people, and my sisters are always at my house. I really really hope you'll understand."

It might have been the first time in my life I was speechless.

"Did I say it wrong?" asked Cassidy softly.

"Uh . . . no. Uh-uh, you said it exactly right."

"Siegelbaum, you're such a good friend," she said.

"Thanks." When she hung up, I was still holding the phone.

How could she do this to me? After nine years of our being best friends, she dumped me for the first boy

26

she ever went out with! Tears welled up in my eyes, but I blinked them back.

I put the phone down — hard. If that was her idea of friendship, I didn't want to be her friend.

Besides, I told myself, shy, sheltered Cassidy had always held me back, always kept me from being as wild as I wanted.

Now I was free.

five

Five

I'm free! I told myself when I woke up the next day: I can do anything I want. I could flirt with boys, I realized seconds later, even go out with them, and Cassidy wouldn't know. I could even call her and say the bet was off. The thing was, though, I definitely needed this "time out" from boys, and the bet would help. I'd stick with it.

I hung out all day with Sonya Rountree and Kelly Vail, really nice girls on my block. Too bad being with them wasn't terrific. Not that it was terrible. It was just that they'd been friends since third grade, so I didn't understand half of what they were saying, and wasn't too interested in the other half. Plus every time they laughed together, I felt crummy.

On Sunday, I went to the skating rink with a bunch of girls from school. I talked, joked, and laughed even more than usual. But I felt lonelier than when I was by myself. And I couldn't even talk much to boys, or I might start to flirt.

School was torture on Monday. No best friend. No boyfriend. I was so bored I raised my hand and answered in class a few times. I ran into Jay Ruiz when I was walking home alone. We'd gone out once. Smart, sweet, and good-looking, he was also vice president of the Student Council. He told me about the town's no-nuke rally, scheduled for the next Saturday afternoon. "It's not the kind of date Archie would take Veronica on," he said, "but want to come with me?"

I actually opened my mouth to say yes, before I remembered the bet. "I can't. But please ask me out again after June twenty-first . . . or I'll ask you, okay?"

Jay laughed. "I hope the Earth's still around."

I kept waking up and telling myself I'd do exciting and adventurous things with fascinating new friends. Only somehow I ended up at home, alone — either in my room, reading or drumming; or in the kitchen, cooking. Friday marked one week without Cassidy. The day started with three kids at my school asking me how come they hadn't seen me, the party girl, at the mall or the movies or any parties, which I responded to by changing the subject. The day ended with my using the fanciest cookbook in the house to make my parents a dinner of Poulet Poêlee aux Aromates, Riz aux Poivrons, and Poires Belle Hélène.

"This is incredible," Jerry said.

"Marvelous," said Elaine.

Then they both put down their forks and looked at me. Uh-oh, I'd gone too far. I never should've cooked an entire meal I couldn't pronounce.

"We're concerned about you, Susanna," Jerry said. "You've been spending so much time at home alone."

29

Elaine said, "We haven't seen Annie around lately. . . ."

I never told my parents that Jeremy'd dumped me. I'd die before I'd tell them Cassidy had. Elaine's eyes were sad, Jerry's forehead creased.

"There's really, truly, absolutely, positively nothing to worry about," I said.

"Why hasn't Annie been over?" Elaine asked.

"And why has the parade of boys stopped?" asked Jerry.

"Simple," I said, thinking frantically. "Annie's been spending lots of time with her boyfriend, Robby."

Both Elaine's and Jerry's faces brightened. And then their mouths opened to ask the next question.

"Which is perfect," I said, before either of them could speak, "because it lets me take a little rest before I start spending lots of time with *my* boyfriend — my new one."

"Oh?" said Elaine, perking up a little.

"We always enjoy meeting your friends," said Jerry.

"You'll meet him soon." I pointed at my parents' plates. "Hey, come on, eat a little something."

I shoved a whole Poire Belle Hélène into my own mouth to shut myself up. A new boyfriend? Where had that come from? And I'd told my parents they'd meet the boy. How in the world could I bring home a boyfriend and also give up guys?

When I got into bed that night, I brought an old friend with me. Not a teddy bear. One of my baby books. I opened *The Look-It-Up Family*, by Kate O'Neill. In this, the first book of the series, the Look-It-Up Family woke one morning, and Little Lowell Look-It-Up immediately began to look up information about the sun, while Mother Look-It-Up looked up the history of clocks, and Father Look-It-Up looked up breakfasts around the world. By the time the family finished looking things up and sharing their information, it was night — and they were still in their pajamas.

If only I could look up what to do now! Instead, I fell into a very fitful sleep.

But inspiration came in school the next day.

In homeroom I was skimming the biology chapter I was supposed to have read carefully the night before, when the bell rang. As I glanced up, Ben Green slid into the room. Literally. Mr. Reading, the teacher, wasn't there yet, and nobody else even blinked. Ben had been sliding into homeroom ever since the baseball team started practicing.

As I looked at him lying on the floor, an idiotic grin on his face, I figured out how I could bring home a boyfriend while giving up guys: I could get Ben Green to pretend to be my boyfriend. Then my parents would be happy, but since there was no chance I'd ever really date, kiss, or flirt with Ben Green, I could still win my bet with Cassidy.

It was Cassidy who'd first told me about Ben. After moving to town two years ago, he went to Saint Al's. Cassidy swore it was true: that at eighth-grade graduation, the nuns inscribed most kids' yearbooks, "Best wishes" or "Good luck," but in Ben's yearbook the principal had written, "May God have mercy on your soul." Then Ben had switched to my school.

Now how could I get him to be my boyfriend? I thought about this as I moved on to social studies.

"I am Mr. Mulgrew," said a mean-looking man, "your substitute teacher today."

31

The class groaned. Ms. Kamrad was practically everybody's favorite teacher. We missed her.

"I will now call the roll," said the sub. He looked at the seating chart, then at the class.

In the first seat of the first row was Todd Dunn, once known as "Meatball" because of his shape. Then Todd took up weight lifting. Now his biceps were so big he could hardly lift his arms to comb his hair, and his new nickname was "Monster."

The sub looked at Monster, at the seating chart, back at Monster. "Tiffany?" he said.

The class rocked with laughter, Ben braying like a horse. It was Ben who'd switched the names on the chart, I'd bet on it.

Betting . . . that made me wonder again how to get Ben to pretend to be my boyfriend. My allowance definitely didn't cover a boyfriend-for-hire. During English — my favorite class, and not just because it was the last of the day — the answer came to me.

After greeting the class, Mrs. Sensi reminded us, "Your book reports are due next Friday." She smiled. "I'm looking forward to reading them." Gesturing toward the blackboard, she said, "Take another look at these suggested authors." She read off the list, beginning with Jane Austen. After she said, "Herman Melville," she looked toward the back of the room. "Ben Green . . . Niko Kolodny . . . you're not allowed to trade baseball cards in English class."

"Baseball cards?" Ben's expression was angelic as he slipped the cards in his jeans pocket. "We were trading literature cards, Mrs. Sensi. I just offered Niko one Herman Melville for two Mark Twains."

The class laughed. Mrs. Sensi didn't, but her eyes

sparkled. "I won't ask you to hand those cards over to me, Ben."

"Thanks," Ben said. "It'd kill me to give up my Herman Melville."

The class laughed louder. Mrs. Sensi's eyes turned thoughtful as she spoke softly, almost sadly. "Ben, you really can't afford to be class clown." I knew the rest, which she didn't say: You might end up going to summer school.

For once, Ben was speechless.

And I was saved.

"Hey, Ben." I caught up with him as he left class.

"Hiya, Susie. Looking good, Susie, baby."

I ignored this. He said stuff like that to all the girls. Sometimes he messed up and said it to teachers. For all I knew, he'd said it to nuns. "Too bad about English class," I said.

"No way I'm going to summer school." Ben took a baseball and glove from his backpack, replaced the backpack, and threw the ball into his glove. *Thwap.* "I've got important stuff to do this summer."

"A job?" I said. "Or is your family going on a big trip?"

The ball went into the glove. *Thwap.* "Baseball."

I walked down the hall with him. "But if you flunk English . . ." I looked up until my eyes met his. He was about six two, more than a foot taller than I. If he pretended to be my boyfriend for long, I'd be in traction.

"I can't flunk," Ben said. "I've got a great book report coming up. On *Moby Dick.*" He smiled smugly.

"Wow, you read *Moby Dick*? That's an incredibly hard book."

"Who said I read it? I just said I'm doing a report on it."

"Oh . . . well, what're you going to say?"

"Bull," Ben replied as he smacked the ball into the glove. "Mainly that Moby Dick was a great man."

I looked at him. "Uh . . . Ben . . ."

"Yeah?" *Thwap* went the ball in the glove.

"Moby Dick was a whale."

Thwap. Thwap. "Quit kidding, Susie." *Thwap.*

"I'm not kidding." I twisted my mouth so I wouldn't laugh.

Ben's eyes narrowed. "What kind of jerk would write a whole book about a whale?"

"Herman Melville," I said.

Ben crossed his eyes.

"Hey, don't worry, I have a proposition."

"Told you I was irresistible," he said, putting his arm around me.

"A serious proposition," I said, unwinding his arm.

"Forget it. I've got baseball practice." He walked out the front door of school.

I ran after him, catching him on the bottom step. "I'll tell you my proposition on the way to baseball practice."

"You really want to watch me practice, right?" He winked and nudged me. "You want to be my athletic supporter."

I refused to react. "I'll tutor you in English if you pretend to be my boyfriend," I said.

He looked down at me. "Say what?"

"It's simple," I said. "See, I bet my best friend — well, she used to be my best friend, but anyway — I bet Annie Cassidy that I could give up guys until summer vacation. But then my parents started worrying because I wasn't going out with boys, so I told them I was, and now I have to bring home a boy and pretend he's my boyfriend." I took a breath. "I know it sounds weird, but . . ."

"Weird's my middle name," Ben said. "Back when Monster was Meatball, he once hired me to be his bodyguard. And I was Tommy Chen's beard."

"What?"

"When private eyes say 'beard,' they mean a disguise, a way to fool people. Tommy's parents said he couldn't go out with Amy DeMaio, because she's not Chinese. So in public the three of us hung out, and I acted like Amy was my girl. But I disappeared a lot."

"That's something like what I want you to do!"

"I've got no time, though. I practice baseball after school two days a week, and next week we'll start playing those two days. After school two other days, I practice cross-country and crew."

"Huh?"

"Running and rowing, Susie. Running and rowing."

"That still leaves one weekday."

"All year I play pickup football with the guys."

I couldn't help making a face. "Don't you ever do anything besides sports?"

He laughed. "It's okay if *you* don't like sports. You're a girl."

"Wait a minute. I could be great at any sport, if I just put my mind to it."

Grinning, he said, "Susie, you gotta put your *body* to it."

"I'll prove I can do sports," I said. "I'll make it part

35

of the deal. After school, I'll run and row with you, and then we can go to my house and I'll tutor you in English."

Ben looked at me for a minute. He sort of snorted. Finally, he stuck out an enormous hand, and we shook. Ow, that hurt. I hoped it wasn't an omen.

Six

After English class the next day, I expected Ben to wait for me, but he walked out of the room. I ran after him. "Ben, I thought we were going to do a sport today."

"Today I play football," Ben said. As we walked down the hall, he took a football from his backpack. He tossed the ball, it spun in the air, and he caught it in the crook of his arm.

I knew zilch about football, but somehow this was hard to admit. "So?" I said. "I can play football."

"You play football, Susie?" He tossed the ball from one hand to the other.

"Well . . ."

"You can block, tackle, kick, run, pass, and receive?"

"Uh . . ."

"You know the wingback formation, the split end,

the double-wingback, the split-T, the wing-T, the 6-2-2-1, the 7-diamond, and the 4-3-3-2?"

With a shrug and a smile, I answered, "Doesn't everybody?"

"Plus the blitz, bomb, red dog, naked reverse, and sudden death?"

Naked reverse? Sudden death? I felt a little sick.

Ben was still tossing the ball back and forth. "And I guess you know the whole history of football, all about the greats, like Bronko Nagurski, Bulldog Turner, and Bruiser Kinard."

"Bronko?" I said. "Bulldog? Bruiser?"

"But probably, like me, you really admire the super-tough guys who've played more recently, like Blood McNally and Mean Joe Green."

"So I can't play football and don't know anything about it," I said. "Big deal." I went on. "But since you told me Weird's your middle name, your football fans must call you Ben Weird Green, right?"

Ben said, "Susie, if you really *could* play, you'd get a nickname sort of like Too-Tall Jones. You'd be Too-Small Siegelbaum."

"It'd be interesting to see the cheerleaders try to spell out Too-Small Siegelbaum," I said.

"Yeah. Halftime would be longer than the game." Ben's hand shot behind his head, as if he were going to throw the football, but he just pretended to. "I'll come over to your house after the game," he finally said.

As I walked home, I realized that Ben was almost always moving — practically in perpetual motion. But his face hardly ever showed any emotion.

Later, when the doorbell rang, I opened the door, smiled, and greeted Ben brightly. "Hi!"

"Hi," Ben said, also smiling. "I wore a necktie so your folks would be impressed with your new boy-friend." The tie was shiny purple, with a pattern of pink flamingos and gold palm trees. He was wearing it over a T-shirt, with jeans and high-tops.

"Thanks a lot," I said.

He looked at the little sign over the doorbell. " 'Dr. E. Siegelbaum . . . J. Siegelbaum . . . S. Siegelbaum.' So your dad's a doctor, huh? And now I'll meet your mom."

"It's my mom who's a . . ."

Ignoring this, Ben came inside, walking with the grace and delicacy of Big Foot. As he passed the living-room mirror, he checked himself out, cocking an eye-brow and smoothing his hair. Besides being tall, he was broad-shouldered, with straight brown hair and blue eyes. But was he good-looking? Who knew? He acted so ridiculous, who cared?

"So, you don't have any second thoughts about our deal?" I asked.

"I never even have first thoughts about anything," Ben said. "You know me, Susie."

I nodded. I knew him — Ben Green, a jock and a clown. "But if you knew me, Ben, you wouldn't call me Susie. I like to be called Susanna. Except Cassidy calls me Siegelbaum. Or anyway, she used to, be-fore . . ."

"Susie's a good name for you," Ben interrupted. "Cute and silly."

"Thanks a *lot*."

"Hey, from me, that's a compliment." Before I could react, Ben put his arm around my waist and grinned down at me. "Since I'm supposed to be your boyfriend, shouldn't we . . . like . . . get physical?"

39

"No!" I said loudly.

He let go immediately. If he hadn't, our deal would've been all off. "Sorry," he mumbled.

"Okay." I was glad he apologized. I hadn't expected him to. Leading him into the kitchen, I said, "I always study in here. I hate to be too far from food."

"Yeah, nothing like a snack before you study," Ben said. "And also while you study and after you study."

I smiled. "That's one thing I agree with you about." As Ben sat down at the table, I poured two tall glasses of apple juice, put two granola bars and two bananas on a plate, and set everything on the table. The phone rang, but when I picked it up and said hello, the caller hung up. I brought napkins to the table and sat down to eat. There was a sip of juice and a bite of granola bar left.

"Got anything else?" Ben asked.

"What's the symbol on your family coat of arms?" I asked. "The crossed knife and fork?"

He laughed. "At our house, my kind of eating's called Hoovering — sucking it in like a Hoover vacuum cleaner."

That made me laugh.

"Susie, I gotta tell you. I can't sit still much longer," he said.

"You've only been sitting still for five minutes, eating the whole time," I said. "You didn't even open a book yet. All you've opened is your mouth."

Ben grinned. "I'm not gonna open a book. I'm just gonna write my book report." He took a pen and paper from his backpack. "But not on *Moby Dick*."

"Oh, then you did have a second thought about something."

About to write, Ben looked at me. "Don't let it get around."

Five minutes later he handed me the paper, which I immediately read. He'd reported on a book called *Wainwright Wagons West*, by D. Butler Bentley. It was a historical novel about a big family's covered-wagon crossing from Pennsylvania to Wyoming in the mid-1800s. He detailed the plot and critiqued the book as "gripping . . . history come alive."

Amazed, I said, "Ben, this is a great book report. And the book sounds so interesting, I'd like to read it. Is it in the school library or the public library?"

"Neither."

"The bookstore at the mall?"

"Nope." Again, he had no expression on his face. "I made it up."

It took a few seconds for that to sink in. "You made up the whole book?" I said. "The title, the author, the plot, and the critique?"

"Yup."

My voice came out very high: "Wouldn't it have been easier to read a book?"

"Not for me," Ben said, standing up. "Reading's against my principles."

As I stared at him, my father came into the room. "Hello, there," he said, smiling warmly and extending his hand to Ben. "I'm Jerry Siegelbaum."

"This is Ben Green," I said.

Ben shook Jerry's hand. "Hey, Dr. Siegelbaum."

"I'm not a doctor," Jerry said, still smiling.

"Elaine's the doctor," I said.

"Huh?" said Ben.

"Elaine's my mother," I explained. "My mother, the doctor."

41

Ben's eyes narrowed.

"I'll start dinner," Jerry said. "How about joining us, Ben? I'm making my famous pesto sauce for the pasta."

Ben's mouth dropped open. "I . . . thanks, but I've gotta go." Without saying so, he clearly thought: This guy's bizarre.

I knew just what Jerry'd do. Instead of getting offended, he'd try to make Ben more comfortable by kidding around. Jerry got this mischievous look on his face. "Yes, Ben, Susanna's mother's a doctor, and her father's . . . well, two days a week I guess you could call me a househusband."

"How about a housespouse?" I suggested.

"Even better," said Jerry.

Ben didn't say anything, he just started to blush!

I didn't want Ben *or* Jerry to feel bad. "Lots of men like to cook, Ben. Arnold Schwarzenegger's a fantastic cook." I'd made that up, but maybe he was.

Ben said, "Is he gonna make a sequel to *The Terminator* called *The Pasta-Maker*?"

Jerry laughed even before I did. "I hope you'll sample my cooking another time," he told Ben.

"Okay, Dr. — Mr. — Jerry." Ben reddened again. "Listen, I've gotta ask you . . ."

Oh, no. Was this going to be embarrassing?

"Go ahead," Jerry said.

"What do you think of my tie?"

Jerry squinted toward the flamingos and palm trees. With a smile, he said, "It's a little subdued for my taste."

Ben grinned. "So long." He walked out the back door.

"Interesting young man," Jerry said, still smiling, before turning back to the stove.

Was Jerry just being nice because he thought Ben was my boyfriend? What did he really think of Ben? What did I really think of Ben? "You know me," Ben had said earlier, and I'd nodded. But now I wasn't so sure. That book report was terrific. Could he be smarter than he seemed?

As I watched Ben walk through the yard, trampling on the new grass, I couldn't think of any answers, just more questions: Could he sit still long enough to keep pretending to be my boyfriend? And to get tutored? Without reading?

And even if he could, could I stand to be around such a goofy guy for two and a half months?

Seven

Bobby Stark, a senior who was captain of both the math and gymnastics teams, and one of the nicest, cutest, smartest boys in my school, came up to me in the cafeteria the next day and asked me to go to the movies on Saturday.

"I'd really really really like to," I said. "But I'm busy."

"How about next Saturday?" he said.

"I'm busy until June twenty-first. Can we get together after that?"

Bobby laughed. "I never heard of a girl dated up two and a half months in advance. Anyway, I'm going to be a camp counselor in Maine this summer, and I have to be there on the twenty-first."

I considered killing myself by eating two portions of the cafeteria's mystery meat.

A couple days later, Ben slid into homeroom and

44

then walked over to my desk. He was wearing a necktie again. Not the shiny purple one with flamingos and palm trees. This one looked exactly like a fish. I stared into the fish's eyes, which gazed back from Ben's middle.

"Hey, Susie, I row today."

"I'll go with you. Then we'll go to my house and I'll tutor you."

We walked to the lake together after school. Somehow the air seemed especially clear. Everything seemed fresh and new. "What a day," I said. "Spring's my favorite season. What's yours?"

"Baseball season," Ben said. "Then football season, basketball season, and hockey season."

"I can't believe you only think about sports," I said, shaking my head. "Remember in the social studies chapter on psychology, we read about free association?"

"I don't remember anything about any class."

"Free association's what psychologists do to find out what's really on somebody's mind. Let's do it, okay? I'll say a word, and you say the first word you think of."

"It's not my kind of game, Susie."

"I know — because you won't sweat. But just try it . . . please?"

"Okay, okay. Go ahead."

Two plump robins were taking a bath in a puddle, which made me smile. "Red," I said.

"Sox."

Ben's sneakers were twice the size of mine. "Your socks are gray," I said.

"Not s-o-c-k-s," he said. "S-o-x . . . the Boston Red Sox . . . a baseball team."

"Oh," I said. "Well . . ." Looking up, I saw fluffy clouds. "White."

"Sox. S-o-x . . . the Chicago White Sox . . . another baseball team."

I rolled my eyes, then met his. "Blue."

"Vida," he said. "V-i-d-a Blue, a pitcher — with the Oakland A's, in his best years. A left-hander. In seventy-one, when he was only twenty-one or -two, he won the Cy Young and MVP awards."

"You win — you only think about sports," I said. We walked on. "I don't know anything about baseball. My parents were big fans when they were kids, though. They say they never got over the Dodgers moving from Brooklyn."

Ben laughed. "The Bums. They were a great team. But they kept losing the World Series to their archrivals, the Yankees."

Crocuses and daffodils were poking their heads up. They were so pretty. Even dandelions were pretty. "My parents usually root for the underdog," I said.

"I'm a Yankees fan myself. The Yanks have been champs more times than any other team," Ben said. "Hey, good thing we're just pretending to be boyfriend and girlfriend, huh? Otherwise, rooting for the Dodgers versus the Yankees, we'd be like Romeo and Juliet."

I looked at him. He'd mentioned something besides sports! To be nice back to him, I did mention sports. "Are your parents Yankees fans, like you?"

"We're here," said Ben.

We were at the lake. The water was such a soft blue, and so smooth. Ben picked up a stone and tossed it in the lake, making ripples that made more ripples. "A plunker," he said.

"What?"

"A stone that sinks without skipping."

"*What?*"

He picked up several stones and threw one. "That was a plink — a long skip." He threw another. "A pittipat — short skips at the end of a long run." Another. "A skronker — a stone that never lands."

I laughed. "What great words. Did your family make them up, like Hoovering?"

"Uh-uh. There's a sport called stone-skipping. There's a society of stone-skippers."

More sports! "Does your family have other made-up words?"

He shrugged, throwing another stone.

"We have lots of family words," I said. "My mother's favorite breakfast is one Jerry and I make on weekends — poached eggs on whole wheat English muffins, which we call 'poachies.' When one of us curls up on the sofa next to the other, we don't call it snuggling or cuddling, we call it 'shnoogling.' And a tight hug isn't a bear hug, it's a bubby hug, because my grandmother's hugs are a lot like a Heimlich maneuver."

Ben was holding a stone, just looking at it.

"I'm going to tell Elaine, Jerry, and Bubby about plinks, plunkers, skronkers, and pittipats. It'll make them laugh. And it'll be more words for Scrabble." That made me think of Cassidy. I picked up a stone and threw it as hard as I could.

"Plunker," Ben said. Then he said, "There she is."

Cassidy? I whipped around. But Ben was pointing at a boat. He walked over and stepped into it. Still wearing my backpack, I followed. When Ben held out his hand, I said, "I can do it."

"Okay." He untied the boat and sat down. The boat swung, I swayed. For a few minutes I tried to balance

47

myself so I could sit down gracefully. Then I fell down.

Ben laughed.

"What kind of boat is this?" I asked.

"A scull. It's for crew, which we don't have at our school, but they do at the Academy." That was the super-fancy school nearby. "I know the head of the phys ed department there. He lets me use this old one they've replaced."

"Why do you want to use it?"

Ben hesitated, looking at the water. "I'm practicing so I can go out for crew in college." He picked up the oars. With sure strokes, he rowed out onto the water.

"Do you practice a lot?" I asked.

"Three times a week for a year. This boat's for two people, but someday I want to do the single scull."

"The single scull sounds like a vicious motorcycle gang."

"Yeah, I guess so. All it means is, you row by yourself about a mile and a quarter as fast as you can."

"Is that hard?"

"Nah. Your back goes out, your legs go numb, and you get bad cramps in your stomach. But you just work harder."

"Ben, if I even scratch my finger, I make myself a sling," I said. "If it hurts, why keep doing it?"

"You're not supposed to even mention the pain. My hero, Mad Dog Loggins, gave his coach another forty all-out strokes at the end of a rough workout — then passed out."

"That's crazy," I said.

"Listen, Susie, you don't know anything about it."

I made a face. "All right, then. While you row, I'll read." Taking my lit text from my backpack, I flipped through it. "Aha — 'The Rime of the Ancient Mariner.' "

48

I read out loud. And read. And read. What a long poem! As the albatross was hung around the mariner's neck, I yawned. "Ben, you'll get more out of this if you read it out loud yourself."

Ben was concentrating totally on rowing.

"Ben? Come on, you read and I'll row."

He blinked, then laughed. "*Who's* gonna row?"

"Who else? Moi. Susanna Siegelbaum, the old salt." I tossed the book his way. How complicated could rowing be?

After looking at me for a few seconds, Ben handed me the oars. Then he picked up the book. " 'When looking westward . . .' "

He was hamming up the reading, acting like a clown. As I struggled with the oars, I thought: If he doesn't know how to do it right, why not just ask for help? The oars weren't doing what I wanted. Maybe something was wrong with them. I struggled on.

A few minutes later, the boat was moving better. I realized I'd been concentrating on rowing when I suddenly heard Ben's voice. He was reading seriously — and it sounded good! He stopped. "Susie . . ."

"You were doing really well," I interrupted. "Keep reading. You . . ."

The boat rammed into a large rock. "Yuch!" I stood up.

"Better take my hand," Ben said, holding it out.

"You think I don't know what I'm doing," I said. The boat rocked, and so did I. "I know what I'm doing." Completely losing my footing, I tipped the boat to one side. "What I'm doing is falling overboard!"

I was under water.

Eight

I swam to the surface. I sputtered, shook my wet hair, and wiped the water from my eyes.

This time when Ben held out his hand, I took it and climbed into the boat. Ben took off his tie, then his shirt. "Here, dry yourself."

After blotting myself, I was still wet and starting to shiver. Ben, in his undershirt, had goose bumps on his arms. He rowed quickly to shore, tied the boat up, and we walked toward home. For a change, I didn't feel like talking. My mouth was moving, anyway, because my teeth were chattering.

"I thought of a couple of made-up words," Ben finally said.

What was he talking about? "Oh — family words."

"Once, when I was little, we lived in an apartment and a grouchy old lady named Martha lived under us. Every time I made a noise, she banged on her ceiling

50

with something, probably a broomstick. Then we moved to another town, another apartment, and this time we were on the first floor, with noisy neighbors over us. The first time my mom banged on the ceiling with a broomstick, I said, "Hey, Mom, now *we're* the Marthas."

I laughed. "So a Martha is somebody who ruins somebody else's fun."

He nodded, and we walked on. "Another time, another apartment, this family lived over us . . . my mom told me there used to be a family on TV called The Whiners, who whined all the time."

"Really?"

"Uh-huh. But this family who lived over us yelled all the time, not just when they were mad. We called them The Yellers. The father was the worst, and we called him Old Yeller."

I laughed again. This was only the second time Ben had mentioned his family. How many apartments, how many towns had they lived in? My family's made-up words were different from his, I thought: Schnoogling and bubby hug both meant cuddling, and poachies were a favorite food; Ben's Marthas, Yellers, and Old Yeller were troublesome neighbors. I looked at Ben, who was cracking his knuckles. When he saw me, he crossed his eyes.

Before we went into my house, I took off my waterlogged sneakers, and Ben took his fish necktie from his jeans pocket, putting it on with his undershirt. Jerry was sitting at the kitchen table, reading the newspaper. He stood up, looking worried. "Susanna, are you all right?"

"Slightly soggy," I said, forcing a smile. How to explain?

"We were researching a paper on *Moby Dick*," Ben said.

"You certainly dressed for it," said Jerry, looking at Ben's fish necktie. He turned to me. "Susanna, what really happened?"

"We were in a boat, and I fell overboard."

After shaking his head briefly, Jerry said, "You'd better dry off, sweetheart." Turning to Ben, he said, "When I was a kid, I thought *Moby Dick* was called *Moby Duck*."

Ben laughed. "Anybody could make a mistake about a nutso name like that, huh, Susie?"

Instead of answering, I blurted, "Hey, you two have the same name as a brand of ice cream — Ben and Jerry."

Ben grinned. "Speaking of ice cream . . ."

"While Susanna dries off and gets changed, I'll see about a snack for all of us," Jerry said, and I left the room.

When I came back, Jerry and Ben were sitting at the kitchen table, each eating a frozen yogurt on a stick, and laughing. Ben said, "The best Yogi saying is, 'Baseball is ninety percent mental. The other half is physical.' "

He and Jerry laughed, and Jerry said, "My favorite is, 'Okay, everybody, pair up in threes.' "

More laughter. "Yogi sure had trouble with numbers," Ben said. "I heard that when a pizza-man asked Yogi whether he wanted his pie cut in six or eight slices, Yogi said, 'Six. I don't think I could eat eight.' "

Jerry and Ben cracked up. Yogi? I thought. It sounded familiar. Yogi Bear? Or a holy man from India?

"We're trading tales of the old Yankees catcher Yogi Berra," Jerry said.

"Sounds like fun," I said, "if you care about baseball." That sounded awful! "I'm sorry — I didn't mean to be a Martha."

Ben laughed, and explained Marthas to Jerry, while I went to the freezer and got myself a frozen yogurt on a stick. When I came back to the table, Ben stood up. "Gotta go."

"We didn't study English," I said.

"We'll do double next time."

"Oh, sure." I rolled my eyes.

" 'Dear Lord!' " he said. " 'It hath a fiendish look!' " Then he walked out.

"What was Ben quoting?" Jerry asked.

" 'The Rime of the Ancient Mariner,' " I said.

"A question occurred to me earlier and I asked Ben," Jerry said. "I asked him why you two haven't gotten together on weekends."

My heart stopped. Somehow I'd never thought of that.

"He told me how his parents are divorced, but he's very close to his father, so he spends every weekend with him."

My heart started again. "Right," I said.

"And I told Ben I was an artist as well as a housespouse."

"What did he say?"

"He said his father's an extremely successful businessman and a great athlete." Jerry looked out the window at Ben, who'd already reached the gate. "As I said, an interesting young man."

He was? Maybe he was! I was a confused young woman.

The phone rang, and I answered it.

"Hi, Siegelbaum, it's me."

Cassidy! I knew who it was from her first word. But I was so mad at her for taking so long to call me, I almost said, "Who?" Instead, I just said, "Hi."

Silence.

"I'm sorry I haven't called, but I've been really busy. Robby and I . . ."

"I'd like to talk, Cassidy," I interrupted her, "but I've got a million things to do." I hung up.

I was a *very* confused young woman.

Nine

The next day at school, Dan Wolff, Gerard O'Malley, and Bill Linder asked me out, a record for a single day. A record for refusals, too. It wasn't exactly fun. Then Kristen Witherington invited me to a party at her house Saturday night.

I couldn't stand saying no again. I decided I could limit my time with guys and still have a great time. "I'd love to go," I said.

"Your friends Annie and Robby are coming," she said.

"Too bad I already made other plans."

I asked Amanda Witt, my biology lab partner, to come to my house and listen to music after school. A transfer from some finishing school, Amanda said she loved rock and roll.

But as we walked home, I found out she didn't like

any of my favorite groups. "They're too white," said the blue-eyed blonde.

"Elvis? The Rolling Stones?" I said. "The Four Tops can't be too white. They're all black guys."

"Their sound isn't soulful enough," Amanda said.

How could I be friends with somebody who thought Levi Stubbs lacked soul? After Amanda left, I played the Tops's "Seven Rooms of Gloom."

Then I went out for a walk. A shower had left puddles, and I remembered how, when Cassidy and I were little, she'd avoided puddles while I'd stomped right through them, laughing. Today I stomped right through a big puddle, splattering my shoes and socks with dirty water. Yuch. What a jerk.

I could see Cassidy's backyard. The lilac tree was in bloom! The smell of lilacs was even better than the smell of freshly baked bread or beef stew simmering the second day. Every April, I plunged my face into the lilacs, inhaling ecstatically. All of a sudden I saw Cassidy in her backyard, and then Robby, right behind her. They were talking and laughing.

I turned away and walked home.

As usual at six o'clock, Elaine was sitting in the kitchen at the big oak table, sipping herb tea. Also as usual, she'd taken off her shoes, even though today she was still wearing her white doctor's coat over her sweater and skirt. Sometimes I pictured Elaine marrying Jerry in a long white dress and veil — and bare feet. "How are you?" she asked, smiling as she lifted her face for a kiss.

"Couldn't be better," I lied.

"Hi, you two." Jerry came into the room, carrying

a bag of groceries, and kissed Elaine and me on the cheek.

"How was your day?" Elaine asked him.

"Don't ask," said Jerry, pouring tea into a mug. He looked so beat, I got up to put away the groceries without being reminded.

After Jerry drank some tea, he grinned. "There was one bright spot," he said. "An old, sad-looking man often stands outside the diner where I usually eat lunch. Most days I give him a dollar. Today he looked worse than ever, and all I had was a five, so I gave it to him." Jerry's eyes were bright. "He told me, 'You're paid up for the week.'"

We all laughed. As Jerry sat down at the table, Elaine said, "You really don't want to talk about the rest of the day?"

He shook his head. "One of the patients was having a rough time." Looking from Elaine to me, he said, "Got any good news? I could use some."

"As a matter of fact," Elaine said, "I have an announcement."

Surprised, I sat at the table, too.

Elaine said, "Today I was offered the job of director of the Women's Center."

"Elaine, congratulations!" Jerry said, beaming.

"Wow!" I said.

Gazing into her mug of tea, Elaine said, "I'm not sure it's for me. It's less medicine and more finding ways for the Center to help even more women." As she looked up, her dark eyes were intense. "But I'd like to try."

"I'm glad," Jerry said, and Elaine reached across the table for his hand.

"Me, too," I said.

Elaine smiled. Then Jerry leaned across the table, Elaine leaned toward him, and they kissed on the lips for several seconds.

Tears filled my eyes. "I was wondering," I found myself saying. "Did you two ever consider divorce?"

My parents looked at me and burst out laughing. Then they looked at each other. "This answer goes for both of us," Jerry said. "Divorce, no. Murder, yes." They cracked up. Somehow I felt even worse.

I was thrilled about Elaine's new job, but somehow all that evening my parents seemed such a *couple*. Even sleeping under the quilt Bubby had made me, I felt cold.

Elaine went to the clinic to work on Saturday — the first time I could remember her working on a weekend. Jerry didn't even mind. He said he was delighted to have time to paint.

I went to the library. Every novel I picked up seemed to be about friendship or love, so I put them all back. Passing the children's room, where Cassidy and I had spent so many hours, I peeked in.

"Is this a good book?" a boy who looked about seven asked me, holding up a fairy tale. Mrs. Bannan, the librarian, was helping another kid fill out a library card, with several kids waiting to pay fines or borrow books.

"I loved it when I was your age," I said.

The boy opened the book to the first page. "There are some hard words."

"Really?" I read that page for him. "Can you read the next page?"

He had trouble with a couple of words, but I helped him sound them out.

"Terrific!" I said.

He smiled. "I'm gonna read it. Thanks for helping me."

Smiling back, I said, "My pleasure."

Walking by the adult nonfiction, I saw a sports section, with lots of books about baseball. I thumbed through a baseball encyclopedia. Hey, nicknames! Football had Bronko, Bulldog, and Bruiser; Blood, Mean, and Too-Tall. Baseball had The Say-Hey Kid, Shoeless Joe, The Splendid Splinter. It also had Spaceman, Dizzy, Dazzy, and Daffy.

I brought home biographies of two baseball greats — Babe Ruth and Ty Cobb. That evening when my parents went to a party, I read about Babe Ruth, baseball's first great home-run hitter. What a character! One player said Ruth "wasn't born, he fell from a tree." Ruth was always chewing tobacco or gum, or smoking cigarettes or cigars; he gambled, drank lots of liquor, and stayed up late in nightclubs; he ate fifteen-egg omelets in one sitting. Yet he was one of the greatest athletes who ever lived. I stayed up late finishing the story of The Sultan of Swat.

The next morning, I started the Ty Cobb biography. How different he was from Babe Ruth! Cobb set so many records for hitting and stealing bases, he was the first person elected to the Baseball Hall of Fame. But he was a tough, mean man, the most hated man in baseball, who fought even with his own teammates. I read the story of his life in one sitting.

My parents rented a Marx Brothers movie Sunday evening, but I needed to work on some school projects. I took out my notes. Hmm . . . for my history paper on a U.S. president, I'd picked John F. Kennedy — the cutest. And for my anthropology elective, I'd outlined a paper on courtship rituals among the Guru-rumba of New Guinea. I wasn't going out with boys, I wasn't kissing them, I wasn't even flirting with them. And if anybody'd asked, I would've sworn I was hardly thinking about them. Ha!

I called Bubby. So she wouldn't worry, I made myself sound cheerful. "Hi!" I practically chirped.

"What's wrong?" Bubby said.

"Nothing. Nothing. Honestly. Nothing." I sighed. "Bubby, can I live with you in Florida?"

"Darling, would you really enjoy living in a retirement community?"

"I'll pretend to be your seventy-year-old little sister. I'll wear your clothes and a white wig."

"You'll be the only one here with white hair. I just dyed mine a new shade, Champagne Bubbles."

I started to laugh, but it became a groan. "Oh, Bubby."

"Susanna, what is it? What's the matter?"

"I don't want to talk about it."

A pause. "How's your friend Annie?"

"Annie who?" When Bubby didn't answer, I said, "She hates my guts. And I hate hers."

"Ah, a normal friendship."

"Hate?"

"Susanna, the opposite of love is not hate. It's in-difference. When you have strong feelings of any kind for somebody, you care about them. And you have so many strong feelings, darling. Just like me. When I was a child, there was a famous French actress, Sarah Bernhardt. I had such strong feelings, and got so dra-matic about them, my father called me Sarah Heart-burn."

I laughed. Then I said, "I'm really mad at Cassidy."

"I'll give you an old Jewish curse to put on her: 'May you grow like an onion with your head in the ground and your feet in the air.'"

"Oh, Bubby, I wouldn't want that to happen to Cassidy."

Her voice soft and soothing, Bubby said, "You think I don't know that, darling?"

"Bubby, I love you."

"I love you, too."

"So what's up with Betty and Beattie?"

"Well, it was starting to look like there should be a book about us called *Betty and Beattie Get Tubby*. After exercising, we were spending the rest of the day talking and eating. So yesterday we found something else to do — we volunteered to work at the city hospital."

"No kidding. What do you do?"

"We give information, deliver flowers and candy. It gives us a good feeling, helping people."

Hanging up, I was smiling. But later, from my bedroom window, I looked out at a downpour. Spring was supposed to be beautiful! In bed, I turned my pillow over, punched it, turned it again. I rolled from my back to my belly to my side.

I really missed going out with boys. I missed being with Cassidy even more. And being with Ben was so weird. I never knew what he'd do or say. Sometimes he was interesting — and nice! — and I wanted to know him better. But he wouldn't let me. He wouldn't even let me tutor him. I was so mixed up, I'd almost rather have been with the Stooges — except not once a week for a year. Oh, why did I make that dumb bet?

From the stereo, Bruce Springsteen stopped shouting "Born in the USA," and James Taylor began to sing a sweet and gentle song, "You've Got a Friend."

To stop myself from blubbering, I tried to think of something good that happened that day. I remembered my talk with Bubby, and how happy she sounded about helping people.

Then I thought about how I'd helped that little kid in the library children's room. The rain kept pounding on the windowpane, but the memory of that one nice moment warmed me and calmed me, made me smile, and let me sleep.

Ten

When I woke up, the sun was shining — and I had an idea. I'd volunteer to work at the library children's room Saturdays or after school. Mrs. Bannan was so busy, she'd be sure to welcome help. I could recommend books. Maybe I could even help kids read.

This was so exciting, I wanted to shout it out. But when I went downstairs, Elaine already had gone to work — she'd been leaving really early since her promotion — and Jerry had that dazed look he always got right before he started painting. Even though the sun was bright, my shoulders slumped all the way to school.

As I walked into the school building, Ben came up to me. "Okay, Susie, the sport of the day is cross-country. In other words, run until you puke."

"What a lovely motto," I said. "Maybe my grandmother would needlepoint it onto a pillow."

He just laughed.

63

At least he didn't get sarcastic back. Hey, maybe *he'd* listen to my idea about the library. "Ben, I was thinking . . ."

"Wow," he said.

That shut me up. He'd never understand anyway.

After school, Ben and I walked to the park. "Ready to run?" he asked.

"Why not? I learned to run right after I learned to walk."

He laughed. "This isn't running for the bus. It's five miles."

Five miles! I thought. "So?" I said.

"For a couple of years, I've been running five miles, four days a week, and eight to ten miles once a week."

I felt like fainting. "So let's run," I said, as we entered the park.

"First we've gotta stretch. Hamstrings, calves, thighs, groin." His eyebrows came together. "Do girls even have groins?"

"Uh . . ." Who knew? "We have loins. Do boys?"

"Maybe we'd better just do it." Ben immediately touched his palms to the ground, repeating it several times.

I bent over. "Ugh." My back cracked. After a struggle, I managed to touch my fingertips to my ankles. "Okay, I'm stretched enough." Ben stretched, and I ached for ten more minutes.

"We'll run on the nature trail," he said. "It turns around and ends up back here."

"Ah, yes, nothing like being at one with nature," I said.

"Watch out for poison ivy, gopher holes, and snakes," Ben said. "Ready . . . set . . . let's go." We took off together.

Within seconds, I fell behind, and with every second, I fell further. I kept running. Breathing heavily, feet hurting, I kept running. Ow! A sharp pain in my chest.

Did he say five miles or fifteen? It seemed like ten already. Soon I was panting, my legs shaking, my feet aching. This was too much like work! Ben was so far ahead, I couldn't even see him. Of course that meant *he* couldn't see *me*.

I slowed down. Then I strolled out of the park, onto the street, and stuck out my thumb. A minute later, a car stopped. The driver was Ezra Pogorsky — a senior at my school — who was nice enough to drop me off near the start of the nature trail.

Ben was waiting. After I'd cheated, he still beat me! Shaking his head and laughing, he said, "You're unbelievable."

"Did you puke?" I asked, to keep him quiet, as we walked together.

"Close," he said. "You're . . ."

"Hey, Ben," I interrupted, so he wouldn't mock me, "how about an English lesson right now? How about some synonyms? I'll bet you can think of ten synonyms for puke."

Ben snorted.

"Come on. One is throw up. Now you say one."

He just looked at me.

"Vomit," I said. When he said nothing, I said, "What — you're afraid to compete? Chicken? A wimp?"

"Barf," he said. "Upchuck. Heave."

"Excellent!" I said.

"Lose your lunch . . . toss your cookies . . . toss your tacos . . . blow your doughnuts."

"Fantastic."

"Ralph," he said.

"Ralph?" I said.

"Woof," he said.

"Woof?" I said.

"Kiss the porcelain god," he said.

"Huh?"

"Puke in the toilet," he explained.

"Oh." I had an odd sensation in my stomach. Not a pain, like when I was running . . . "How colorful," I said.

"You think that's colorful?" said Ben. "Here comes the best." Eyes wide and shining, he said, "The Technicolor yawn."

"Yuch." I turned my head and put my hand over my mouth.

"Gross," Ben said. A few seconds later, he passed his shirt over my shoulders. "Practically every time I've been with you, Susie, I've ended up giving you the shirt off my back."

"I came close, but I didn't really throw up," I said, handing his shirt back to him. "You and your running," I muttered.

"You didn't almost puke from running, Susie. You almost puked from giving me an English lesson about puking."

I looked at him. He was right, but I wouldn't admit it. Leaving the park, we walked toward my house. "Babe Ruth never got sick," I said. "Even after a midnight snack of six eggs, a platter of pigs' knuckles, and six beers, he'd play the next day — and hit a homer."

Laughing, Ben turned to me. "How'd you know that?"

"I just read Ruth's biography. Ty Cobb's, too."

He looked at me as if I were from Mars. "How come?"

"You talk so much about sports, I got curious." I didn't say I was also avoiding stories about love and friendship.

Ben was quiet for a minute. Then: "Ruth and Cobb were tops, the best — great, great athletes."

"Yeah." I stared at the crack coming up in the sidewalk. "But they weren't really good people, were they? I mean, in a way, Ruth didn't have any brains, and Cobb didn't have any heart."

"You don't know what you're talking about!" Ben reached up, pulled a new leaf from a tree, and flung it into the street.

I didn't say a word for a while. Then I spoke softly. "Maybe I don't. Or maybe I'm not saying it right. But there's a Yiddish word my grandmother uses for a good person. The word is mensch and it means someone with integrity, honor, and dignity."

"Let me get this straight, Susie," Ben said. "I'm supposed to care what you think your grandmother would call the two greatest stars in the history of baseball — and she's not even speaking English?"

My face got warm. "Ben, do you want to be a great athlete?"

Silence. Then: "Yeah . . . what do you want to be?"

"Lately, a rock star." I tried to think of a rock star with integrity, honor, and dignity. Hmmm. . . . Luckily, we were home.

Ben and I went inside, and Jerry looked up from his newspaper. "Susanna, you're pale. Don't you feel well?"

"We were running through the park, and my stomach got upset, but I'm okay now." I went upstairs to the bathroom, where I washed my face and brushed my teeth. When I came back to the kitchen, Jerry and Ben were sitting at the table.

"How about Lou Gehrig?" Jerry was saying.

"I know him," I said. "He was a great baseball player, called the Iron Horse because he played in so many consecutive games. I read about him in Ruth's and Cobb's biographies, and once on TV I saw an old movie about him — *Pride of the Yankees*. He batted .300 or more for 12 years in a row, and drove in 100 or more runs for 13 straight years. He was the Most Valuable Player 4 times. But . . ."

"Susanna," Jerry said, but there was so much more I wanted to say.

"Even though he was terrific, he was pretty much overshadowed by Babe Ruth. Plus some people said he was a Mama's boy because his mother even traveled with him on the team bus. He died really young from a disease that has a big, long, Latin name, but now it's usually called Lou Gehrig's disease. And . . ."

"Susanna," Jerry said softly, "I was asking *Ben*."

My face felt hot as Ben stood up and said, "Gotta go."

"We didn't do any English homework!" I said. I quickly unzipped my backpack and pulled out the gigantic English textbook.

"So long," Ben said.

"See you, Ben," said Jerry.

As Ben walked out the back door, I ran after him, still holding my big, fat English book. I blurted out to his back: "Hey, Ben, why won't you let me tutor you?

That was our deal, and now you won't do it. You're going to flunk English."

Walking faster, he went right out the gate. I followed him. Clutching my English book close to my heart, I said, "It would be a shame if you flunked English, don't you think?"

He stopped and turned around. "Nope. I don't think. Ever."

"Ben, that's not true. But how come you goof so much?"

He looked right at me. "Hey, Susie, how come *you* do?"

That surprised me. He wasn't the only one who liked to make people laugh. But I wasn't going to say so. Instead, I asked, "Were you always funny?"

"Were you?" he asked.

I should've known he wouldn't answer. "My parents say I was. They say I made up my first joke when I was three and a half. A Good Humor truck came down the street, and I wanted to ride in it, but Elaine said if I did, all the kids would want to, and Jerry said, 'Then what would we have?' So I said, 'A Good Human truck.' "

Ben laughed. He reached up and started to pull a leaf from a tree, then lowered his head. "You think all humans are good?"

I looked at him. "Don't you?" Suddenly my eyes got wet.

"What's wrong?" Ben's voice was less gruff than usual.

"I miss Cassidy," I blurted. "We only fought once before, I don't even remember what about. I only remember how we made up. I was riding by her house on my bike, with my nose in the air, the bike hit a rock, and I fell off. Cassidy ran right over and asked if I was okay. I said, 'A friend in need is a friend indeed,' and we started giggling like crazy."

"Isn't that your friend now?" Ben said, pointing up the street.

Cassidy and Robby were walking together. *Hey! Hi! I wanted to yell. How are you? I miss you!* When Cassidy looked at me, my arm shot up and my mouth opened. But she looked away and spoke to Robby, who kissed her on the cheek.

"Did you see?" I said to Ben. "Kissing! On the street!"

Ben laughed. "Who's talking? A Martha? Or Susie Siegelbaum, who's gone out with almost every guy in school except me?"

My face flaming, I said, "I'm better off without Cassidy. She's so shy and sheltered and scared."

"She didn't look shy or sheltered or scared to me," Ben said. He looked directly into my eyes. "Susie, you're jealous."

"What?!" I shook my English book. I'd never hit anybody, never would. I just shook my book at him.

"Jealous," he repeated, reaching out to grab the book.

I pulled the book toward me. Ben pulled it toward him. Back and forth we pulled, in a tug of war. Then Ben suddenly let go, and the momentum made me push the book with all my might right in his face. As the book fell to the sidewalk, blood appeared on Ben's mouth.

Eleven

I ran to him. "Ben, I'm so sorry. I didn't mean to hurt you. Please try to keep calm." My voice was shaking.

"Susie," Ben said calmly, "I'm okay."

"Sure you are," I said, my voice still shaking. "But I have to get you to the hospital emergency room, just in case." I didn't mention the blood, because I didn't want him to panic.

He touched his mouth, getting blood on his hand. He touched his teeth. Calmly, he said, "I'm bleeding, and my two front teeth are loose."

"Don't panic!" I said, close to tears. I quickly removed the old white shirt of Jerry's I was wearing over a T-shirt, folded it, and very, very gently blotted the blood. More blood instantly appeared.

"I can do it," Ben muttered, holding the shirt to his mouth. "This has happened to me before. I mean,

71

I never got hit by a book before. But once I was playing football and somehow my mouth came in contact with Monster's head. Another time I was playing baseball, catching without a mask, and a hard ball hit me in the same place. The dentist at the hospital, Dr. Blumenfeld, is like an old pal by now."

What a relief. I was still worried, though. "I'd better tell your parents before I get you to the hospital. Are they home now?"

Ben hesitated, then said, "My mother's out of town."

"How about your father?"

He blotted some blood, looked at the stain, folded the shirt again, and put it back against his mouth. I remembered how he'd told Jerry he was close to his father, the great businessman and athlete. "I haven't seen my father in fourteen years," Ben said. "So I wouldn't know him if I did see him."

How awful! I felt sick to my stomach. I had to think straight, though. I thought again of Ben's mother, which made me think of Elaine. "Maybe I should take you to my mom."

"Is she a dentist?" His voice was muffled by the shirt now.

"A gynecologist."

He made a weird sound. A laugh! I could tell by his eyes.

So much for thinking straight. "Ben, stay where you are, I'll be right back." I ran home and told Jerry, "I . . . I . . . Ben got hurt. His mouth is bleeding, and two teeth are loose."

"Where is he?" Jerry asked, already standing and checking in his pants pockets for his keys. I told him, we got in the car, and drove to Ben. He got inside. "What happened?" Jerry asked, as we drove off.

I said, "I . . ."

Ben interrupted. "I was showing off, doing cart-wheels on the street. Susie said to quit, but I didn't, and I fell on my face."

"Ben . . ." I said.

"I'll be fine, Jerry," Ben said. He told Jerry about the other times he'd hurt his mouth and teeth.

While Jerry parked the car, I walked with Ben to the emergency room. His mouth had stopped bleeding. Handing me my shirt, he said, "Hey, this time *you* gave me the shirt off *your* back."

Lots of people were in the emergency room. Entering, Ben called, "Yo, Adrian." He *did* look like Rocky after a bad bout, and people laughed.

As Jerry joined us, a nurse handed him a paper and pen. "Please sign this permission form for your son's treatment," she said, then walked away.

Ben's lips hardly moved when he whispered, "My mom's out of town." He paused. "My dad, too."

"Who's responsible for you?" Jerry asked, his voice also low and his forehead wrinkled.

"Me," Ben said.

"You're staying alone?" The wrinkles multiplied.

"I'm a big guy," Ben said.

Jerry looked at him for a minute. Finally, he signed.

"Thanks," Ben said. "Thanks a lot."

Jerry looked as if he was about to say something, but the nurse came over for the form.

"You guys don't have to hang around," Ben said.

"I'm staying," Jerry said, in a no-nonsense tone.

"We're staying," I said.

A tall, skinny man wearing a white coat came into the room, and Ben called, "Hey, Dr. Blumenfeld, how's it going?"

"Oh, no. Not you again, Ben," the dentist said. "Not another sports injury."

"I'm trying for a record."

"Quite a son you've got there," Dr. Blumenfeld told Jerry.

After a second's hesitation, Jerry said, "I know. But sometimes I wish he'd give up sports and take up the violin."

"Time to go to the dental clinic," Ben said. To Jerry and me, he said, "Really, go home . . ."

"We're going with you," Jerry said.

All the way to the dental clinic, Ben made jokes. He also made jokes in the dental chair. Even when the dentist used a very long needle to give him several injections in the gums, Ben made jokes. Even after the dentist said, "This will hurt," using his fingers to push the two front teeth back where they belonged.

"Didn't hurt at all," Ben said. "I'm a totally macho guy."

"And a comedian," said Dr. Blumenfeld. "And who's this — your sister or your girlfriend?" He pointed a needle at me.

"Does she look like my sister?" Ben said.

As Dr. Blumenfeld looked, I thought for sure he'd say, No, but she looks like your father.

"No," Dr. Blumenfeld said. "She's a lot prettier."

Ben winked at me.

Dr. Blumenfeld put a temporary brace on Ben's teeth, to hold them in place, and said, "Please, Ben, take up chess."

On the way home, Jerry drove even more cautiously than usual. "You were brave," he told Ben.

"Nah. I'm a devout coward." Ben gave an exaggerated yawn. "But I've done this so much, it's boring."

"I suppose your parents have told you to be more careful," Jerry said.

"It's come up," said Ben.

In the silence that followed, I looked out the window. It was dark now, but the sky was studded with stars.

"How about staying at our house for dinner?" Jerry said. "I promise to make a soufflé instead of a steak."

"Thanks. I've gotta go home, though."

"I don't like to see you go home alone," said Jerry.

"I'm not gonna like to see myself, period. Any minute my upper lip is gonna be swollen." Ben looked in the mirror. "Uh-oh. It's already swollen."

I blurted: "Your upper lip looks like a duck's beak. You look like a duck."

"You look like you *should've* ducked," said Jerry.

I quickly looked at him. Did he know about the book? He was only kidding, though, just making a pun.

"I look like I've got a strange mallardy," Ben said.

"Very good pun," Jerry said, laughing.

"I don't get it," I said.

"A malady is a disease, and a mallard is a duck," Jerry said.

Ben said, "Jerry, thanks for pretending to be my feather . . . I mean, father."

Jerry said, "Listen, if you want to come over later, Ben, just give me a wing . . . I mean, ring."

With a groan, I said, "Will you guys please quit

making duck puns?" Oh, no, I was being a Martha! "If you don't stop," I said right away, "I'll quack up."

Jerry and Ben cracked up.

"Ben, we'd like to have you for dinner, and the night," Jerry said when he'd stopped the car in front of Ben's house.

"My mom'll be home soon," Ben said. "If you get the hospital bill, give it to me, okay? And thanks again for everything."

"You're welcome." Jerry smiled.

"I'll walk you to the door," I told Ben. Outside, I said, "I'm sorry. You really were incredibly brave. And it was my fault, but you didn't tell on me. Thank you."

"Hey, we both pulled on the book," he said. "But just remember, when we did the three R's together — rowing, running, and reading — the one that got me into the emergency room was reading." He wiggled his eyebrows.

I laughed. Then I got serious. "Ben . . . another thing. You were right. I'm jealous of Cassidy."

"Who's perfect — except me?" Ben said. He pulled a ring of keys from his jeans pocket. "Check this out." Not only keys were attached to the ring. There was also a small plastic replica of a dead chicken.

"Too bad it's not a dead duck," I said.

Ben laughed. "I just thought of a great nickname for me, with this lip."

"What?" I asked, already starting to smile.

"Moby Duck," he said.

I was laughing as Ben stepped inside the house, turned on the light, and closed the door.

"I like Ben a lot," said Jerry as we drove home.

"Me, too," I said.

Jerry laughed. "Of course. He's your boyfriend."

No more than he's your son, I thought.

"Do you know much about his family?" Jerry asked.

"Nope . . . hey, look, was that a shooting star?" It wasn't. I just had to change the subject.

Setting the table for dinner, I thought again that Ben was right — I was jealous of Cassidy. How awful I'd felt when Ben had said it; and how relieved, after admitting it was true. I looked out the window. I could almost see Cassidy's house. If only I could be her friend again! But what if she didn't want to be mine? I'd die!

While we ate dinner, Jerry told Elaine what had happened to Ben. He said Ben had been brave, kind, warm, and modest. And funny, of course. Plus, he was smart, I thought. So why was he class clown? Why was he failing English? Why did he act like a comic-book jock, all brawn and no brains?

As Elaine served Jerry's homemade brownies, I thought of Ben's father leaving when Ben was a baby. It was bad enough for Cassidy, who was eleven when her father was killed. But Ben couldn't even remember his father.

I remembered pretending to play chess with Jerry when I was only about three. He'd say, "Uh-oh, Susanna's going to capture my king." I'd grab his king and run. He'd chase me, catch me, and whirl me around in his arms.

"I'll be coming home from work earlier, starting next week," Elaine said. "Shall we drink to that?"

"By all means," said Jerry, with a broad smile.

"Hooray!" I said. I hoisted my cup of hot chocolate, and it was met by Elaine's mug of herb tea and Jerry's glass of skim milk.

I thought about Babe Ruth's family life. His hardworking parents owned a saloon. At age seven, Babe Ruth played hookey, roaming the streets with tough kids, maybe chewing tobacco, drinking whiskey, and stealing. Seven years old! When he was eight, his parents said they couldn't handle him, and put him in a combination orphanage and reform school.

Ty Cobb's father was a state senator — a smart, stern man Ty Cobb could never seem to please. When Cobb made the major leagues, his father congratulated him by saying, "Don't come home a failure." Soon after, Cobb's mother shot and killed his father, saying she'd mistaken him for a burglar.

That night as I lay in bed under Bubby's beautiful quilt, I thought how lucky I was, what an easy, happy life I had. My parents were terrific, and so was Bubby. And Cassidy'd been such a good friend I'd never needed another. Until now.

I threw off the covers, walked to the window, and opened it wider. Chilly! But the air was also refreshing, invigorating. And I'd never seen so many stars. I couldn't wait for tomorrow.

Twelve

I woke up early the next morning and when Ben arrived at school, I was waiting for him at the door. "How are you?" I asked.

"Just ducky," he said.

I laughed. His lip was even more swollen. "You don't look so bad," I lied.

"You don't look so bad yourself," he said, wiggling his eyebrows and flicking an imaginary ash from an imaginary cigar, like Groucho Marx.

"Want to get together after school tomorrow?" I asked.

"Yeah, but you don't have to run or row with me, Susanna. I'll just come over to your house when I'm done."

"Hey, great," I said. It wasn't until we walked into homeroom that I realized he'd called me Susanna, instead of Susie.

At lunchtime, I made a date with Sonya and Kelly to go to the mall on Saturday.

After school, I went right to the public library, walked into the children's room, and volunteered to help. Mrs. Bannan, who'd known me for about ten years, asked me just one question: "When can you start?" With a grin, I said, "Right now."

I checked books out, put returned books back on the shelves, showed one kid how to find the book she wanted, told another kid what a book was about — without giving away a surprise in the plot.

"Do you have a book about grammas?" asked a boy around seven years old.

"Sure," I said.

"My gramma had very close veins," he said.

He had to mean varicose veins. I tried not to laugh.

"My gramma died," the little boy said, slipping his thumb into his mouth.

I found him a book about a grandmother who died, and sat next to him while he read it. As soon as he finished, he turned back to page one and began again. I felt really good.

When I got home, I called Bubby, told her about my volunteer job, and asked about Betty.

"She's very well, but . . ." Bubby hesitated. "Darling, I'll tell you a secret. I met a nice man in aerobics class. His name is Sam Straus, but I call him Sam-You-Made-the-Pants-Too-Long."

"Why do you call him that?"

"Because of the song, naturally." Then she laughed. "Sometimes I forget you're not seventy-five years old. There's an old song with that name, about a tailor who makes that mistake." She sang some of it. "It's obvious where you get your musical talent, right, darling?"

Bubby had the worst voice I'd ever heard! Instead of answering her question, I said, "So, are you friends with Sam Straus?"

"I think so, but it's a little tricky. Betty is jealous. She says, 'Go ahead, Beattie, enjoy yourself.' Then every time Sam and I are together for five minutes, she gets peeved."

"Oh," was all I could say.

"Betty's a delightful person. I only hope she doesn't make me choose between her and Sam. Maybe I'd choose her, but I'd miss Sam. As much as I like Betty, I don't want to kiss her on the lips."

"Bubby!" I felt my face turn red.

"Darling, I'm sorry if I embarrassed you."

I laughed.

The next day, as I opened the door to let Ben in, I saw that his lip was still swollen. I thought again of Bubby saying, "As much as I like Betty, I don't want to kiss her on the lips." I blushed and laughed all over again.

"Are you laughing at my lip?" Ben asked. Of course this made me laugh more. "Dethpicable!" he said, like Daffy Duck, and I laughed harder.

I was smiling when we walked into the kitchen and I got us brownies and milk. Jerry soon joined us, and he and Ben started talking about baseball. For a while, I just sat back, looking and listening. The sun streamed in, amazingly bright for that time of day, and birds called to each other, as Ben and Jerry talked.

Jerry smiled a lot. Ben sat still, and the expression on his face changed a dozen times. It was nice to see them both enjoying themselves. Plus I learned about baseball. I learned Jerry was a Mets fan!

Ben was surprised, too. "Susanna said you rooted for the underdog," he said.

"That's how the Mets started," Jerry said. "Their first season, '62, they set a record by losing 120 of 160 games."

"Hey, you're right. I forgot about that," said Ben.

"They didn't get the nickname Amazin' because they were so good. It was because they were so unbelievably bad." Jerry chuckled. "For instance, the legendary Marv Throneberry . . ."

"Marvelous Marv!" Ben said, grinning. "A Met who once hit a line drive and ran to third but forgot to touch first or second, so was called out." After they laughed about that, Ben said, "Jerry, you're a Yankees-hater, right?"

Jerry shook his head. "There's a lot to admire about the Yankees. And I'm a fan of the game more than of any team."

A little while later, as Ben and I went over compound, complex, and compound-complex sentences in our English grammar, Jerry started cooking his fabulous vegetable soup. "Want a taste?" Jerry asked, after the stew had been simmering, and the incredible aroma of butter, onions, herbs, and other vegetables was wafting through the room.

I leapt up. "Mmm, delicious . . . but it needs more pepper."

Ben walked over and gazed suspiciously into the pot. "There's green stuff in there. I never eat anything green."

Jerry just smiled and sipped from the ladle.

"I remember the book about the Look-It-Up Family cooking together," I said. "They looked up information about every ingredient and never got around to cooking, much less eating."

"Listen, I gotta go," Ben said all of a sudden. He walked over to the table and picked up his backpack.

"Ben, we've hardly done any homework," I said. "I hate to be a Martha, but we have to write a newspaper from some historical period by next week. Since I'm already taking Latin, I figured I'd do an ancient Roman newspaper. Want to do it together?"

Ben crossed his eyes.

"How about staying for dinner? We can work on the paper after."

Ben put his backpack over his shoulder, then let it down to the floor. It went up again . . . and down. "Okay."

"Hooray!" I cheered. Ben went into the living room to call home.

When he came back, Elaine was walking in the back door. "At last I get to meet you," she said, smiling as she shook Ben's hand. I was a tiny bit nervous that Ben would act goofy, but he smiled and talked to Elaine like a normal person. And then he actually helped me set the table!

"This is great bread," Ben said after we were all sitting down and he'd bitten into a thick slice of nutty whole wheat bread.

"Made it myself, from my mother-in-law's recipe," Jerry said.

Ben reddened. "I never met a guy like you," he blurted.

Laughing, Jerry said, "At your age I'd never met a guy like me, either. My mother did all the cooking at our house. And I definitely didn't know any artists. My father was a businessman."

"No kidding." Ben leaned forward. "What kind of business?"

"He manufactured women's lingerie. Or, as Papa sometimes put it, 'I'm in ladies underwear.' That usually got a laugh."

"Didn't he want you to go into his business?" Ben asked.

"You'd better believe it. He had me working in the factory after school from the time I was ten. Fortunately for me, I was a disaster at every job."

I didn't know that! My father a disaster? Impossible!

Jerry went on. "The only way I survived working for Papa was, when the other workers took breaks for cigarettes or snacks, I drew. I think I drew everything and everyone in that factory."

"I love hearing about when you were my age," I said.

"I remember a sketch I made of your mother when she wasn't much older than you are now," said Jerry.

Elaine looked toward Ben and me. "On our first date, we went out for pizza, and Jerry drew my face on a paper napkin."

Jerry laughed. "Elaine looked at it and said, 'You didn't make my eyes wider, my nose narrower, or my jaw less strong.' "

"You were disappointed?" I asked Elaine.

"I was delighted," she said. "I knew Jerry liked me just as I am." My parents smiled at each other.

"How about a game of Scrabble after dinner?" Jerry asked Ben.

Ben would say, "No way," I was sure of it.

"You're on," Ben said.

A little later, I laughed at Ben's first Scrabble word. "Chortle? Who ever heard of chortle?" I said.

"It's chuckle and snort put together," Ben said.

"Like this." He snorted and chuckled at the same time. Weird!

"You made it up," I said.

"Lewis Carroll made it up," Elaine said. "It's from *Through the Looking-Glass*, part of the poem 'Jabberwocky.' "

"Oh, right," Jerry said. "You know it, Susanna. ' 'Twas brillig, and the slithy toves/Did gyre and gimble in the wabe . . .' "

I did know it. But how did Ben know it? Over the next hour, I found out that Ben knew a lot of unusual words — enough to beat us Siegelbaums at Scrabble! Of course, we demanded a rematch.

"The English project!" I said, remembering. "We should at least get started, Ben."

"Elaine and I have an exciting evening ahead, balancing our checkbook," Jerry said. He smiled at Ben. "I hope you'll stay for dinner again."

"Yes, often," said Elaine.

I found myself hoping so, too. I looked at Ben, who was smiling. As soon as my parents left, he leaned over the table and began writing fast. No more than five minutes later, he handed the paper to me.

I read: "CLASSIFIED: FOR SALE: Practically new II-horse chariot, owned by little old lady from Venezia. Asking MCCCL gold pieces, horses not included. See Honest Marcus at Honest Marcus's Chariot and Restaurant.

"LOST: Lion, approximately V ft. high at shoulder, yellow-brown, moody, likes raw meat, answers to "Chuckles." Escaped from Coliseum last Wed. Speak to Brutus Exploitum, Coliseum manager.

"FOUND: Lion, approximately V ft. high at shoulder and getting bigger, yellow-brown, no sense of

85

humor. Speak to Cassius Carpathian at Carpathian Day Care Center as soon as possible. Reward expected.

"LOST: Child, about II ft. high at shoulder, II years old. Answers to 'Juvenal.' Last seen leaving for Carpathian Day Care Center Thurs. morning. Speak to Spartacus and Minerva Junius."

Laughing, I said, "Did you just make those up? They're so funny. Morbid, but funny." I looked into Ben's eyes, which were clear and blue. "Ben, you can really write." Excited, I went on. "This is going to be fun. What could the paper be called? I know — *The Roman Times*, of course. What would that be in Latin? Let's see . . . I guess *Roma Tempi*. We'll do news and feature stories, for sure. And an editorial. And sports — like the Gladiators at the Coliseum. Hey, even comics. Snoopy could daydream about being a charioteer at Circus Maximus. Garfield could *invent* lasagna. What else? A fashion page, with the latest in tunics, togas, and sandals." I grinned up at Ben. "Okay, let's get started. I'll do the sports. . . ."

"Ha-ha."

"Kidding, of course. You do the sports and features, and I'll do the . . ."

"You do the whole thing, Susanna."

"Ha-ha yourself."

"Everything's gotta be your way," Ben said.

"It does?" My voice went up an octave in a second.

Laughing, he said, "Are you kidding? You've gotta be the center of attention, you've gotta know all the answers, and you've gotta make up all the rules."

Ben picked up his backpack and took the paper from my hands. Without another word, he walked out.

Thirteen

I held my hand out, although there was no longer any paper in it. Then my fingers folded into a fist. Ben was crazy! First he was a clown and a jock, then a really nice boy, and now a nut.

Shouting a quick good-night to my parents, I went to my room, undressed, put on pajamas, and flopped into bed. I punched my pillow. I had to be the center of attention, know all the answers, make all the rules? Ridiculous! I just wanted to do the newspaper right, and Ben wanted to goof, as usual. He acted as if he were *trying* to flunk English. So let him!

The next day at school, I acted as if Ben didn't exist. It wasn't hard because whenever I got a glimpse of him, he acted as if *I* didn't exist. I acted cool, confident, and carefree. I knew he saw me. I knew *he* knew I knew.

The only problem was, I felt lonely — so lonely that

in bio, I leaned over my test tube and asked Amanda what singers she *did* like. She invited me to come to her house after school and listen to her James Brown tapes. "Sure," I said. I didn't mention that I couldn't stand James Brown. Not that I'd heard a lot of him, but I definitely didn't like him.

At lunchtime, Sonya and Kelly and I talked about the trip we were taking to the mall on Saturday. "We go to all the big stores," Sonya said, as Kelly nodded. I smiled, but inside I was saying, Yuch. Big stores gave me sensory overload. I got crazy deciding what to look at next. I wanted to go to little stores. Maybe I could come down with a cold and forget the mall. I sniffled several times.

After school at the library, I recommended a Look-It-Up Family book to a little boy who said, "I hate the Look-It-Up Family's guts." I glowered at him and went home early.

The azalea bushes were in bloom, their flowers bright purple, red, and pink. Birds were chirping. The stupid sun was shining. When you felt rotten, there was nothing worse than flowers, birds, and sunshine, nothing worse than spring. As soon as I got home I ate a pint of chocolate-chip ice cream, without even sitting down.

Then I went to my room and drummed along with Chuck Berry's "Rock and Roll Music." But my stomach started to hurt. And that wasn't all. I felt an awful ache deep down inside me as I realized that Ben was at least partly right: A lot of the time I did want to be the center of attention, know the answers, and make up the rules.

I remembered how I was always doing things like yelling out "Heathcliff," even though it embarrassed

Cassidy. I remembered how I'd acted like a know-it-all about boys. I remembered how I'd pretended to Ben that I knew about sports, how I'd never admitted he was right about my clowning as much as he did, how he'd ended up in the hospital before I admitted he was right that I was jealous of Cassidy. And, yes, I'd tried to take over the Latin newspaper.

I'd never felt so lousy in my life. Or so alone. Wrapping my arms around one of my drums, I lay my head down on it. Not very comforting. My kaleidoscope, the one Cassidy'd given me on my seventh birthday, caught my eye. I got up, picked up the kaleidoscope, and aimed it at the light. As I looked through it and turned it, colors and shapes rearranged themselves into different patterns. It was mysterious, fascinating, and beautiful. My all-time favorite present. I started to cry, then stopped myself.

I reached for the phone and dialed. "Hi, it's me — Siegelbaum." There was silence. "Cassidy, I'm sorry I didn't call back sooner. I've missed you."

"Can you come over and talk?" Cassidy asked.

In no time I was running over to her house. How weird to run up her porch steps again — and how nice. While I was taking a deep breath before knocking on the door, I saw Cassidy in the doorway, as if she'd been waiting for me. "Hi," she said, with a little smile.

"Hi!" We both just stood there. Then I came forward at the same time she came out of the house, and I got hit in the head with the screen door.

"Siegelbaum, are you all right?" She sounded really worried.

My hand on my head, I laughed. "A friend in need is a friend indeed."

"You remember that?" she said, with an enormous smile.

I nodded about seven times, smiling back at her, and we sat on the top step. Then she looked one way and I looked the other. I pulled my knees up to my chest and wound my arms around them. She stretched out her legs. I put my legs down and crossed them, uncrossed them, crossed them the other way.

"Siegelbaum . . ." she said, at the same time I said, "Cassidy . . ."

We laughed, and she said, "You first."

"I'm really really sorry I hung up on you and didn't call you back. The truth is . . ." I took a very deep breath. "I was jealous of you and Robby."

Cassidy looked right at me. "I was wrong to take so long to call you. And after you didn't call back, I called you, but when you answered, I chickened out and hung up." She sighed. "Then I saw you — and you shook your fist and started to yell at me."

"I wasn't shaking my fist, I was waving! I was going to yell, 'Hi! I miss you!' "

"Really?" Her voice was small. "If only I'd known . . ."

My sigh was deep. "I've found out some stuff about myself in the last few weeks. Not such hot stuff."

"What do you mean?"

"For instance, that a lot of the time I want to be the center of attention, know all the answers, and make all the rules . . . right?"

"Well . . . I wouldn't say that."

I smiled, but not for long. "What would you say?"

"That . . . um . . . you do act like you're a star, somebody special, with . . . I don't know, sort of a glow around you."

I didn't say a word for a minute. Then I moaned, "How could you be friends with me for so long?"

She smiled. "I want to say this exactly right." After looking at the sky, she looked at me. "You *do* have kind of a glow around you. And it's always made *me* feel brighter."

"Oh, Cassidy!" I blubbered.

"Actually, your glow has *made* me brighter," she said. "You're so warm and funny and smart and talented and generous. You're the most interesting person I've ever known. And I'm a better person for knowing you."

"Oh, Cassidy!"

"But lately," she said, "I've also been a better person because of Robby. I've been speaking up more, since *he* thinks *I'm* interesting, and . . ."

"You *are* interesting. You've always been," I said. "Who said you weren't? I . . ."

"Will you please let me finish?" she said.

"Sorry," I said.

"I . . ." she began.

"But I want you to know that I think you're more interesting than I think you think I think you are!" I said.

"Shut up, Siegelbaum!" she screamed.

"Cassidy!" I gasped.

"What I was trying to say," she yelled, "was like it when we each speak up sometimes and each be quiet sometimes."

"Oh," I said, as softly as I'd ever spoken.

Cassidy held her hand on her heart until she calmed down. Then she also spoke softly. "I learned something else from Robby. I learned I'm basically a shy, quiet person with everybody. And I'd like to change. I'd like to go wild once in a while."

I held up my palm. "I promise I'll still be your friend if you go ape now and then."

She laughed. "Thank you."

We sat side by side, not talking. Then: "Cassidy, I never said this to anybody before, but I'd like to . . . to stop entertaining everybody all the time."

She smiled as her palm went up. "I promise I'll still be your friend if someday you dare to be dull."

"Hey, thanks." Laughing, I said, "What a motto: 'Dare to be dull.' "

We laughed together. In my whole life, I was never so glad Annie Cassidy was my friend.

Fourteen

"Where's Robby?" I asked Cassidy.

"Baseball practice." She looked at the part of the lawn where violets grew. "Siegelbaum, even though I like Robby a lot, I'm just not ready to go steady with anybody."

I didn't say a word.

"The problem is, I don't know how to tell him."

"It's hard," I said.

Two minutes later, Cassidy said, "Thanks, Siegelbaum."

"What'd I do? I just listened."

"I know. Thanks." She smiled at me, and I smiled back.

"Hey, Susanna!" "Hi, Susanna!" "Susanna-Banana!" Jane, Lisa, and Chrissy tumbled out the front door.

"Susanna, teach me to wrestle?" Jane said. "Robby doesn't have time to show me karate since he and Annie started kissing so much."

"Jane . . ." Cassidy groaned.

Lisa interrupted. "Susanna, I'm sick of piano. Will you show me some ballet? Please please please?"

"Hey, Susanna, come play with Lulu and me," said Chrissy.

"Who's Lulu?" I asked. "And where's T.T.?"

"T.T. is D.E.A.D.," said Jane.

"And Lulu's an icky old lizard," said Lisa.

Chrissy held the lizard near my lips. "Kiss her."

"Thanks, I'll just shake her tail." I shook. "Yaaaaaaa!" The tail broke off in my hand.

"That's okay, she'll grow a new one," Chrissy said as I tossed aside the tail, and Jane and Lisa giggled.

"Siegelbaum, I wish we could talk more, but I have to clean up the kitchen and start dinner before my mother gets home — which is any minute," Cassidy said.

Now I could be a friend in need. "Go do that, Cassidy. I'll watch your sisters out here. It'll be a sneak preview of what happens if I lose our bet."

"The bet!" she said. "I almost forgot about it. Have you really stayed away from boys?"

"No dates, no kisses, and no flirting."

"Wow," she said, wide-eyed.

After she went inside, I thought of a great thing to do with the Stooges. I ran inside and upstairs to Cassidy's room, and back. Sitting the Stooges around me on the porch steps, I began to read them *Little Women*. From the first sentence, everybody got into it — including me. We hung on every word I read about motherly Meg, tomboy Jo, vain Amy, and shy, sweet Beth.

"I'm just like Beth," said Chrissy.

"Sure — and Hulk Hogan's like Pee-wee Herman," Jane said, as Lisa giggled. I quickly read the next sentence, bringing us back into the story.

"What a lovely picture," said Mrs. Cassidy, walking up to the porch from the sidewalk. Cassidy came out of the house, and all the girls greeted their mother. "I won't be joining you for dinner this once," Mrs. Cassidy said. "I'm taking a quick shower, changing, and leaving a bit early for my accounting class." She sort of floated into the house.

"Mom's been acting weird since she started the accounting class," Jane said.

"Oh, by the way," said Mrs. Cassidy, looking out the screen door. "You'll all be meeting my accounting teacher soon. His name is Henry Eliot and he'll be coming to dinner."

"How come?" Chrissy asked.

Mrs. Cassidy blushed a little. "Well, for the last few weeks Henry and I have been chatting before and after class. I'd like you girls to know him, too."

Lisa chanted, "Mom's in love with Henry, Mom's in love with . . ."

"Mom, you have a crush on your teacher?" Cassidy squealed. "How embarrassing!"

Amazed, I turned to her. Just months ago, Cassidy'd had a mad crush on her English teacher, Mr. Angelucci. You'd think she'd understand.

"Embarrassing? It's disgusting," Jane said.

"Thrilling!" said Lisa.

"We don't care one way or the other, do we, Lulu?" Chrissy asked her lizard.

"Susanna?" Mrs. Cassidy's face was pink, her eyes bright, and a smile starting. "It's not like you to withhold your opinion."

I hadn't been the center of attention — and I hadn't even noticed! "I think it's terrific," I said.

Lisa sighed, Chrissy kissed Lulu, Jane belched, Cassidy rolled her eyes, and Mrs. Cassidy floated away.

"Quit that stupid sighing," Jane said, punching Lisa.

"Don't you dare punch me!" said Lisa, pinching Jane.

Jane aimed a kick at Lisa, who backed away, knocking down Chrissy, who jumped up and punched Jane and then Lisa in the stomach. All the Stooges were yelling, crying, or both.

"Isn't this a wonderful preview of what it would be like to take care of my sisters?" Cassidy asked me.

"I've gotta win that bet," I said.

And I had to talk to Ben.

As I walked home, it began to rain a little. More of a mist, really. It made everything seem to shimmer. It felt so good being friends with Cassidy again. I wanted to thank Ben for telling me the truth about myself — at least some of the truth. And I wanted to thank him for teaching me that I didn't want to entertain people all the time. Not that he meant to teach me that. But seeing him clowning, I wanted to stop him — and stop myself.

My house seemed like a beacon of light. Coming around the back, through the garden, I saw Elaine and Jerry in the kitchen. Jerry was chopping vegetables in his precise, patient way. Elaine was sitting at the table, her hands wrapped around her mug of tea. She said something — just a few words — and he said a few words back. They laughed.

Ben didn't clown with Jerry or Elaine, I thought. He especially liked Jerry. Then I remembered the last time Ben was at my house with my family. After taking a step closer to all of us, he'd done more than take two steps away — he'd done a backflip right through the door. Was my attitude so totally obnoxious? Or was it something else? It seemed like he just didn't want to be my friend. He wouldn't even look at me. What if I talked to him and he wouldn't talk back?

The next morning when Cassidy and I met, she said, with a smile, "Well, what's new with *you?*"

"Nothing much," I said. "Just that my parents started questioning me about not having a boyfriend, so I said I had a new one, and then they said they wanted to meet him, so I asked a boy to pretend to be my boyfriend, and in exchange I said I'd tutor him in English."

Cassidy had that mono-eyebrow look again. But soon her brain processed that information. "What boy is pretending to be your boyfriend?"

"Ben Green."

"Ben Green?" Now her eyebrows separated and each went way up. "Ben 'May God Have Mercy on Your Soul' Green?"

"Yup." Shrugging, I said, "I know it's hard to believe, but he's really nice. Smart, too. And he gets along great with my parents, especially Jerry."

"Really?" That Cassidy squeak.

"Uh-huh. It's worked out amazingly well. Except, of course, for the time I fell in the lake, and the time I almost threw up all over him, and the time I hit him in the mouth with my English book and he ended up in the emergency room."

"Oh?"

"And the last time he was at my house, when he walked away saying I always wanted to be the center of attention, know all the answers, and make all the rules."

"It was Ben Green who told you that?"

"Uh-huh."

After staring at me for what seemed like a long time, Cassidy said, "Siegelbaum, you really like Ben, don't you?"

"I really do," I said. And she smiled, understanding.

At school, it was one of those bizarre days when I actually learned some stuff, and after school, I had a good time helping out in the library.

Amanda and I went to her house the next day after school. Fancy! I felt at home in her room, though, because even though it was twice the size of mine, it was exactly as messy. We listened to James Brown. He wasn't as bad as I'd thought. The more I listened, in fact, the more I liked him. When I told Amanda, she said maybe she'd listen again to the groups I liked. Walking home, I sang, "Say it loud, 'I'm black and I'm proud.' "

I went to the mall with Sonya and Kelly on Saturday. As we walked into the first big store, I imagined every item falling down on me. "Listen, would you two mind if I went to that little antique-clothes store, Second Thoughts, instead? We could meet in an hour someplace else." Kelly said no problem, and Sonya suggested we meet at Stuff 'n' Nonsense, which sold what Cassidy's family called knickknacks, and mine called chatchkas. I had fun wandering by myself among the old things, and Sonya, Kelly, and I had fun together with the goofy things at Stuff 'n' Nonsense. We each bought writing paper that looked like food — Kelly, a hamburger; Sonya, a hot dog; and me, an ice-cream sundae.

Over the next week, I hung out sometimes with Cassidy, sometimes with Sonya and Kelly, and sometimes with Amanda. At the library, I introduced myself to the kids who came a lot, and found out their names.

Jay Ruiz walked me home from school late in the week. We talked about everything from nuclear war to Saturday-morning cartoons. I didn't flirt with him, or want to kiss him, or go out with him. I just enjoyed being with him.

I was having a terrific time.

There was just one problem: I missed Ben. I really did. When I saw him in school, I tried to stay cool yet get his attention, by doing things like wiggling my eyebrows. Once he glanced at me, and I crossed my eyes. Too bad that after I uncrossed them, he was gone. He kept avoiding or ignoring me.

He was less of a clown in class, though. He stopped sliding into homeroom, and in English he was actually handing in homework. Once he even raised his hand and answered a question — correctly. Mrs. Sensi looked like she might faint.

I told Elaine and Jerry that Ben hadn't been coming over because he had a cold. Elaine said she hoped he'd come to dinner again soon, so we could all play Scrabble. Jerry said he missed Ben. I did, too. How could I let Ben know how much I wanted to be his friend, if he wouldn't even acknowledge that I existed?

One morning that light bulb flashed on over my head again.

Fifteen

A few days later I walked into homeroom wearing jeans, sneakers, and a couple of items I picked up at Second Thoughts — a Yankees cap and a flannel shirt. Kids laughed, and Ben did look at me. But he immediately looked away.

In English the day after, I had to read my book report on a biography. My report was on *The Mick*, by Mickey Mantle of the Yankees. When I looked at Ben, he yawned.

Everybody had to diagram a famous quotation during English on Friday. I picked a quote from the famous Yankees manager, Casey Stengel: "There comes a time in every man's life, and I've had plenty of them." Afterward, I looked right at Ben and smiled. Chewing gum, he blew a big bubble.

I wasn't surprised when it started pouring rain just

as I walked out of school. Then I saw an umbrella —
a big black one — with Cassidy under it. I ran over
to her and under the umbrella. "Hey, Cassidy, it's great
to see you. It's been such a lousy . . ."

Her face was wet. Not with rain, with tears. And
Cassidy almost never cried.

"What's the matter?" I asked, touching her arm.

She just stood there, crying.

"Here, I'll hold the umbrella." She let me take it.
As I put my other arm around her, she put her head
down and said something. "Cassidy, I'm sorry, I can't
hear you."

Lifting her head, she sniffled, then swallowed. She
looked at me. "Remember . . . remember how I said
I wasn't ready to go steady with Robby, but I didn't
know how to tell him?"

"Sure."

"*He* just told *me*."

"Huh?" I didn't get it. Then I did. "Robby told you
that *he* wasn't ready to go steady?"

"Yes." A tear slid down her cheek. Another. Another.

"Oh, Cassidy." I squeezed her shoulder. I almost
said, Cheer up, this is what you wanted — not to go
steady! But I remembered how I'd felt when Jeremy
dumped me for Jessica. And I hardly knew Jeremy.
"I'm really sorry," I said softly.

She nodded, still crying. The rain kept coming
down. "I have to pick up my sisters," she said.

"I'll go with you." Slowly, we walked toward Saint
Al's, as I held the umbrella over us. Cassidy stepped
in a puddle, without even noticing. A truck zoomed
by and splashed water from the curb on us, and I yelled,

"Hey!" but she hardly flinched. A few blocks later, she did stop crying, though. She trudged on silently, looking straight ahead.

It was hard not to tell Cassidy what I thought and felt. It was hard not to tell her what, in my opinion, *she* should think and feel.

We were almost at Saint Al's when she finally said something. "Mr. Angelucci rejected me," she said, her voice thin and flat. "Now Robby." The rain coming down like a curtain, she said, "Maybe I'll become a nun."

I looked at her carefully. Was she serious?

"I'd miss you, though, Siegelbaum. Would you become one with me?"

She was definitely kidding. She must feel a little better! "I'd rather be pope," I kidded back. "He's got so many terrific outfits."

Cassidy giggled. Then she looked confused. A few seconds later, she took a tissue from her pocket and blew her nose. "I know Robby didn't really reject me. He likes me as much as I like him. And I don't want to go steady, either. But . . ." She let out an enormous sigh. "Oh, Siegelbaum, Robby's my first boyfriend."

I just nodded.

"And I . . . I . . ."

I just waited.

As her eyes filled with tears again, my eyes filled up, too. She took another tissue and silently blew her nose. I took the tissue from her and blew mine — which sounded like a trumpet. She laughed. "Look!" she said, then pointed up the street at a teenage boy.

"So?" I said.

"That cute boy walked near us, and you didn't even notice."

I shrugged.

"You've changed!"

"I have?" I looked at my watch. "I almost forgot. I told Mrs. Bannan I'd help at the library today. But if you want to talk more, or . . ."

"I'm really fine now," Cassidy said.

"Are you sure?"

With a quick nod, she said, "Thanks to you."

"You're welcome." I spotted something on the lawn behind her. "Hey, look," I said, pointing. "The first roses of summer."

She turned around. "They're so pretty."

Some of the delicate pink flowers were opening up, and some were about to open. The rain suddenly stopped. I put down the umbrella and handed it to Cassidy. "We've got the whole summer ahead of us," I said.

"Mm-hm . . . and only three weeks to go on our bet. It's amazing that you haven't gone out with, kissed, or flirted with even one boy."

"Yeah, I guess it is."

"Siegelbaum, you really have changed."

"Maybe I have." Another look at my watch. "I don't want to worry Mrs. Bannan. I'd better get going." Cassidy and I smiled at each other.

Walking to the library, I saw more roses . . . boys playing softball, girls jumping Double Dutch . . . an old man and a woman, gardening together . . . Mark Owens, a boy from my homeroom, who called out hi to me . . . a robin . . . I remembered then that Mark and I once went out . . . I saw an oak tree.

All of a sudden, I realized what made me look at boys differently. It was getting to know Ben a little. I had to try again to show Ben that I really wanted to be his friend!

A few days later every kid in English class had to recite a poem of his or her choice. Other girls recited the works of Emily Dickinson, Shakespeare, Elizabeth Barrett Browning. I recited "Casey at the Bat" — in my Yankees shirt and cap. "There is no joy in Mudville," I said solemnly, removing my cap and placing it over my heart. "Mighty Casey has struck out." The class applauded, whistled, and cheered. All except Ben.

Like Casey, I'd struck out.

I walked out of school with my head down, staring at the cold stone steps.

Sixteen

Mrs. Bannan said she wanted to catch up on ordering books, so I should check books in and out and collect fines.

The first kid who came up to the desk was a boy around ten I'd never seen before. He returned a book that was a year overdue. He owed more than the book cost. Searching through his pockets, he came up with a Don Mattingly baseball card, a wad of well-chewed bubble gum, a dead ant, a lot of lint, and three pennies.

I wrote a note to his parents, saying how much he still owed. He pushed the note way down into his pocket, then put back the baseball card, ant, and lint. He put the gum in his mouth.

Matthew, a regular who was also around ten, brought back his book on time. But it was stained with what looked like blood, sweat, tears, and peanut butter and jelly. Plus it had the permanently puckered pages that came from reading in the bathtub.

"Matthew . . ." I said.

"I didn't do anything!" he said. "I didn't do anything!"

"What'd he do?" asked Bobby, the nine-year-old regular in back of him.

"Something bad," announced Andrea, behind Bobby. "Something very very bad."

"Is the library lady going to arrest him?" Bobby asked.

Andrea said, "First she needs a warrant."

Trying to ignore this, I repeated, "Matthew . . ."

"I didn't drop my book in the bathtub!" Matthew said.

"Oh, no!" Bobby gasped. "He dropped his book in the bathtub!"

Andrea said, "He did not. He threw the book in the bathtub. He was very very angry when his mother said he had to take a bath, and he went very very crazy and threw the book into the bathtub."

"Wait a minute," I said. "Matthew was probably just reading in the tub and the book fell in. It could happen to anybody."

"Nothing happened to anybody!" Matthew said.

"Hey, Matthew, it's easy to read a book in the bathtub," Bobby said. "Just keep the book on the side of the tub."

"Yeah, sure, only when you take your hands out of the water to turn the page, you get the book all wet." Matthew was crying.

"Matthew," Bobby patiently explained, "you *never* put your hands in the *water*."

I blinked at Bobby, who was well-read but unwashed. I wrote a note to Matthew's parents, saying that the library would have to replace the book, and telling how much it would cost.

"And after he took the book out of the bathtub," said Andrea, "he threw it at his little sister."

A woman came in, carrying a sleeping infant in a pouch. "What books would you recommend for Jillian?" she asked me. "She's only six months old, but she's extremely gifted."

I wasn't gifted enough to answer that question. "Oh, Mrs. Bannan . . ." I sang out. When she came to the desk, she said I could read to kids, if I wanted. Hooray! Right away, a woman walked over to me, holding a really little kid by the hand.

"Chris is eighteen months old and he just loves trains," she said. "Do you have any books about trains for children this young?"

I found *The Little Engine That Could.* "I'm not sure he'll like it. How about if I read it to him a little, to get his reaction?" I said.

"What a wonderful idea," said the woman. "I'll go upstairs and find some books for myself while you do that."

She sat Chris on my lap. He was really cute — plump, brown-skinned, with soft baby hair, a powdery baby smell . . . and baby slobber coming continually from his mouth. I liked holding him, but wished I were wearing a raincoat.

I started to read. Would he appreciate the story? He looked intently at the book, and his face brightened whenever I said, "I think I can, I think I can, I think I can." At the end of the story, he smiled. Then he opened his mouth, and along with some slobber, out came a word: "Again."

What a compliment! I read the book a second time, putting even more feeling into it, especially, "I think I can, I think I can, I think I can." Chris smiled all through, and laughed at the end. I was proud of myself. "Again," Chris said, clear as a bell.

I looked around for Chris's mother, but she wasn't in sight. So I read the book for a third time. Laurence Olivier couldn't have put more into Hamlet's "To be or not to be" than I put into the little engine's "I think I can." When I finished, Chris clapped! Then he said, "Again."

I stared at him. I sighed. "Chris," I said, "I don't think I can, I don't think I can, I don't think I can."

Chris screamed bloody murder.

Boy, was I glad when the library closed. I practically ran out of the building.

"Watch out!" a deep voice called.

Something was coming at me. A rubber ball!

I started to duck, then changed my mind and reached out for it. Caught it!

At the bottom of the steps, on the sidewalk in front of the library, was Ben. His face was expressionless, and he didn't say a word. I looked silently at him for a few seconds, then threw the ball back. Catching it easily, he sent it back, in a lazy overhand, to me. We tossed the ball back and forth again and again.

Then Ben asked, "Want to go to the lake?"

"Sure." I remembered falling overboard, but didn't mention it.

"This time'll be different, Susanna," said Ben, breaking into a grin.

I smiled back at him. From the corner phone booth, I called home and asked Jerry if it was okay to come home late.

Not long after, Ben and I were at the lake, and a few minutes after that we were *on* the lake. Ben rowed out to the middle, then put up the oars. He sat with his long legs extended. I sat like a yogi — an Indian holy man, not the baseball catcher. We looked around.

The sky was pale blue, with big white clouds, the water was lots of shades of blue and green. On shore, bright wildflowers swayed slightly in the breeze.

Ben and I didn't talk or touch or look at each other. But I felt so close to him. I felt as if we were both part of everything, and everything was part of us.

"What did Huck Finn say about being on that raft?" Ben said. "That other places seemed cramped and smothery, but not a raft? That you felt free and easy and comfortable on a raft?"

"Uh-huh," I said, amazed that Ben should say that.

"Susanna?"

When I looked at him, he was looking at the water.

"I'm sorry I said all that stuff about you. The stuff about you always . . . uh . . ."

"Having to be the center of attention, know all the answers, and make all the rules?" I said.

"Yeah," he said.

"I already forgot it."

He laughed, and I did, too.

"Really, Ben, I'm glad you told me that. You were right, and I've been trying to cut that stuff out."

"I exaggerated. You don't do it all the time. Anyhow . . ." He stopped, then started again. "Anyhow, I do it a lot myself."

I thought about that for a minute. "Thanks for saying so."

Ben looked at me. I thought he'd make a joke, but his eyes, a much deeper blue than the sky, even

109

brighter and clearer than the lake, were serious. "You're really something, Susanna."

"Thanks," I said. "I think you are, too." We both quickly looked back at the water.

"The way you kept trying to tutor me . . . introducing me to your folks and having me to dinner . . . trying to get my attention with the baseball stuff. You've made me feel like . . . like *you've* been paying attention to *me*."

"Yeah, well, even though I was supposed to be your tutor, I probably learned more from you than vice versa. Ask me who the all-time, top-ten home-run hitters are. Go ahead."

"Okay, but first ask me some synonyms for vomit. Like throw up, heave, barf, upchuck, toss your cookies, lose your lunch, blow your donuts, kiss the porcelain god . . ."

"Ralph and woof," I said. "I learned those from you. And I'll never forget the Technicolor yawn."

We laughed. Afterward we were quiet for a long time. Without talking at all, Ben rowed us back to shore and walked me to my house. "Want to come in?" I asked. "Elaine and Jerry keep telling me they miss you."

"I can't tonight," he said, leaving it open for other nights. Very lightly, Ben punched me in the shoulder, the way guys did to each other. I looked up into his eyes and almost made a joke. Instead, I held out my hand. Ben hesitated. Would he do something goofy?

His hand felt strong and warm.

Seventeen

Ben and I began to hang out. Every day his face showed more expressions. In school, he was a little less goofy, and with me — even though we both made plenty of jokes — a lot less goofy. He didn't talk much about himself. But day by day, he let me know him better.

One afternoon we climbed a hill and picnicked at the top. Hoovering a baguette of French bread, a jug of lemonade, and lots of fruit and cheese, we checked out nature. When some birds flew over us, I sighed. "I read someplace that the way a group of geese is called a gaggle, a group of larks has a special name. I can't remember the name, just that it's beautiful."

"An exaltation," Ben said.

"That's right. An exaltation of larks."

"A group of crows is a murder, and a group of rhinos is a crash," Ben said.

"Fantastic names."

"Yeah, and there are some great names for baby animals — a swan's a cygnet, a pigeon's a squeaker. The best is the kangaroo — a joey."

"I love that." I looked at Ben, hoping he'd tell me how he knew all that. When he didn't, I told him about the little boy named Joey who came to the library a lot, but never read. "Joey said his mom makes him come while she gets books for herself in the adult section. He sits there surrounded by books, and never even glances at one."

"Wow, a kid who doesn't want to read — really weird." Ben's blue eyes were so bright when he was kidding me.

Ben showed a lot of expressions at my house, especially when Jerry was around. At the kitchen table, they made up baseball all-star teams for every decade since the sport began. Then, at Ben's suggestion, they made up all-star teams of only short players, only overweight players, and only players with big noses. I was glad no guy made all three teams!

Ben and Jerry got along so well that I started feeling funny about it. Left out. When I realized I was jealous again, I had to laugh. Maybe I'd get jealous my whole life, but at least now I knew what to expect.

One afternoon when I brought a pitcher of iced tea to the table, Jerry was showing Ben how to do origami — Japanese paper folding. I'd seen Jerry make frogs, skiers, and lots of other things without glue or scissors, just by folding little pieces of paper. He'd tried several times to show me how, but I'd always messed up right away, giving up soon after.

After Jerry made a dinosaur, Ben tried to make one, too. His big hands carefully folded the paper smaller

112

and smaller. "Almost," Jerry said, when it didn't turn out. He showed Ben where he'd gone wrong. Ben began again. Who would've thought such a big guy could be so patient? Who would've thought he'd ever want to do such delicate work? "You did it," Jerry said simply, with a smile, when Ben succeeded.

Ben smiled, too. "When I was real little, I was nuts about dinosaurs."

"Tyrannosaurus rex?" I asked.

"Nah. No meat-eaters. My favorite was Diplodocus."

"Wasn't that the longest?" Jerry asked.

"Yeah. Some were ninety feet. But plant-eaters. And goofy-looking. The doofus of dinosaurs."

We all laughed. "That sounds like one of those words for groups you were telling me," I said to Ben. "A murder of crows, a crash of rhinos, an exaltation of larks . . . and a doofus of dinosaurs."

"Susanna, you remembered them all," Ben said, with a huge smile.

Ben and I hung out with Cassidy a few times. After Robby'd told her he wasn't ready to go steady, they'd both said they'd stay friends and even go out sometimes. But Cassidy was avoiding Robby. They'd already finished the last edition of *The Voice*, and she spent most of her spare time reading and writing poems so she could try out for the literary magazine next year. She missed Robby, though. Lots of her poems were about being hurt. I was glad Ben and I could make her laugh.

But when Cassidy and Ben talked on about their days at Saint Al's, getting nostalgic about Sister Mary Magdalen's mustache, I got jealous. I wanted to say: Promise you won't like each other more than you like me! I laughed at myself again. Still, I was relieved that Cassidy knew even less than I about sports. She asked Ben questions like, "Why aren't the Toronto Maple Leafs called the Toronto Maple *Leaves?*"

I introduced Ben to the Stooges.

"Hey, Ben, want to meet my pal Lulu?" Chrissy said.

"Oh, no." Ben laughed loudly.

Chrissy had dressed Lulu in an outfit borrowed from Lisa's Barbie doll — black satin evening gown, fur stole, and red wig.

Ben laughed so hard, his eyes were tearing.

"Lulu's a dumb pet," said Jane.

"She can't sit up or beg or do any tricks at all," said Lisa.

"I bet she can play dead," Ben said.

Chrissy lay Lulu on the sidewalk in front of the Cassidys' house. "She can play dead. See?"

We all looked down at Lulu; then Cassidy, Ben, and I looked at one another. Cassidy bit her lip. Ben crossed his eyes. "Chrissy," I said, very softly. "I don't think Lulu's *playing* dead."

It was Ben's idea to bury Lulu in the backyard. Lisa insisted the lizard be laid to rest wearing Barbie's basic black evening gown, although she took back the fur and wig. Jane found a casket — an empty box of Celestial Seasonings tea.

"Celestial makes sense," Ben said. "It means heavenly."

Chrissy smiled and sniffled at the same time.

Cassidy and I made a little cardboard gravestone. I had some ideas for epitaphs, since I once did a term paper on them. My favorite was: "Here lies an atheist/ all dressed up/and no place to go." But we ended up just writing "Lulu the Lizard, RIP" in fancy letters. Ben dug the grave.

When Chrissy tearfully asked who would say something nice about Lulu, there were no volunteers — until Ben raised his hand. He stood and faced us, looking dignified and sincere.

"Okay, so Lulu was small and slimy," he began.

Chrissy sniffled.

"Even for a reptile, she was run-of-the-mill, no star, no Tyrannosaurus rex."

Several sniffles.

"She was special, though, to Chrissy, Lisa, Jane . . ."

"She wasn't special to me," Jane called out.

"Do you always have to be so mean?" whined Lisa.

"Shut up!" yelled Cassidy, and her sisters were so surprised, they did shut up.

"Like I was saying," Ben said, "Lulu was special to some people. She was special to the people who loved her. And those people will miss her."

Chrissy sobbed, loudly blew her nose, then said, "I wonder what pet I can get next?"

One bad day at the library didn't stop me from going back. The first week Ben and I hung out, he walked me there after school, then went on to do sports. Next day I always told him what happened. When I mentioned Joey again — how he still sat with his arms folded, waiting for his mother, refusing to read — Ben said, "So what? When he wants to read, he'll read."

I thought about that. "You could be right. But Joey's not giving reading a try is like . . . like somebody who's starving not even sampling the food at a banquet."

Ben laughed. "I like the way you said that." The next afternoon he went with me to the library. He took *The Look-It-Up Family* from the shelf, sat near Joey, leaned back, and read. A few times he laughed out loud. When Ben was finished, he left the book on the table, called out, "So long, Susanna, I'm gonna play baseball," and walked out.

Less than five minutes later, Joey walked over to *The Look-It-Up Family*. Sitting down and leaning back, exactly like Ben, he read the book. He laughed out loud. After he read it a couple more times, he came up to me. "Got any more books by this arthur?" I was so glad to say yes, I didn't even tell him the word was "author."

The next afternoon, Mrs. Bannan came up to me as soon as I walked into the room. "Susanna, I have some good news. I've gotten several phone calls from parents of children who visit this library. The children have enjoyed your reading to them. It gave me an idea I'd like to pursue, if you'll agree."

"What is it?"

"Every Saturday, I'd like to have a formal story hour. You'd be the reader, the Story Lady. We'd plan the books ahead of time, put up posters outside the library and in the schools, even a weekly notice in the newspaper. I've thought before of doing it myself. But frankly, I'm not a performer. Would you be timid?"

"Me? Timid about performing? Are you kidding, Mrs. Bannan?"

She smiled, and her eyes sparkled. "Yes, I am, Susanna."

"It would be fun to read to lots of kids once a week," I said.

As Mrs. Bannan and I began to make plans, I got

really excited. I could put lots of feeling into reading, and make the books come alive for the kids. Mrs. Bannan said we should pick out three for me to read — one for kids up to six, one for kids from six to nine, and one for older kids. She said they should all appeal both to kids who loved reading, and to kids whose parents dragged them, kicking and screaming, to the library. A challenge!

When Mrs. Bannan said a reporter and photographer from the local newspaper would be coming to the first Story Hour, I got even more excited. This was something like being a rock star! Elaine and Jerry said they'd come, and Ben, and Cassidy. Her sisters said they'd come and be quiet — except at the end, when they'd cheer, applaud, and scream "Bravo!" Sonya and Kelly said they'd come, and also Amanda. If only Bubby could.

Calling Bubby on her seventy-seventh birthday, I was eager to tell her about Story Hour. After I sang "Happy Birthday," she said, "Darling, thank you for the birthday presents. The earrings are gorgeous, the poem is magnificent — I'm so happy you wrote it yourself. And as for the new Tom Selleck poster I asked for, I'm the only one at the retirement community who has it." She sighed. "Your parents called earlier. I suppose you know what they sent me."

"Elaine said you asked for candy."

"Diet candy they sent. I'm not sure I want to live much longer if it means eating diet candy."

"Oh, Bubby." I wished she wouldn't kid about dying.

"That mother of yours was born sensible, Susanna. In grade school in the 1950s, when other little girls wanted to be stewardesses or movie stars, she wanted to be a doctor. She'd come home from school, I'd be watching wrestling on TV, enjoying a little snack . . . say, a piece of cheesecake. Elaine would take an apple and a glass of milk, and go to her room to do her homework."

"Bubby, do you think my daughter will be like that?"

"Oy," she moaned. Then: "If you're wondering how Betty and Sam are, they're marvelous. In fact, they're in love." Bubby paused. "With each other." She sighed.

My sigh echoed hers. "Bubby, why is life so complicated?"

"To tell you the answer, I'll tell you a joke," she said. "A man asked his rabbi: 'Why do Jews always answer a question with a question?' And the rabbi answered, 'Why not?' "

"So the question 'Why is life so complicated?' gets the answer 'Why not?' " I smiled, shaking my head. "Bubby, I love you."

After we hung up, I realized I'd forgotten to mention my being Story Lady. It could wait.

The phone rang, and I answered it.

"Susanna, it's Ben. There's something I've wanted to do for a while, only I didn't have the guts."

"Really?" What could he mean? Windsurfing? Skydiving?

"Okay, here goes," he said. "Want to come to my house for dinner?"

Laughing, I said, "I'd love to. But that took guts? How come?"

"You'll find out," Ben said.

Eighteen

It was between day and night, light and dark, when I walked over to Ben's for dinner. Spring was almost over, summer about to begin. I could smell roses.

I pictured the inside of Ben's house as looking like the Baseball Hall of Fame: cases filled with sports trophies and plaques, framed autographs of sports stars, statues of Babe Ruth and Ty Cobb, and Ben's first spiked shoes — bronzed.

After I rang the bell, Ben opened the door, gulped, and said what sounded like "Ha" but must've been "Hi." He stepped aside so I could come in. Funny, his house smelled like *my* house. Or was I imagining it? What was that nice aroma?

Ben looked nice, too, in his white polo shirt and jeans, without a silly tie, or an arrow in his head. Over the last couple of weeks I'd noticed what a great face he had. Not movie-star handsome — most people would probably say his nose was too long, and his mouth too wide — but very appealing. Those blue eyes were beautiful, too.

But now their expression was super-serious. Like a pitcher staring down the guy at bat. I almost expected to see his mother signaling him, like Yogi Berra.

As Ben led me into the living room, his mother walked in from a room beyond. She didn't look like Yogi Berra. Tall and slim, with short, gray hair, she wore a simple cotton sweater and skirt, and sandals. Her nose was long, and her mouth wide. Her eyes were gray. Somehow, she looked delicate.

"Susanna, how nice to meet you at last," she said. She smiled as she extended her hand. For somebody who looked delicate, she had a powerful voice and a heck of a grip.

"Please sit down," she said, and as we did I glanced around the living room. One whole wall was covered with shelves, and every shelf was crammed with books — thousands of them. There was hardly anything else in the room. The walls were white, there were no plants, and just a few pieces of furniture. Not the Baseball Hall of Fame.

"Wow, Mrs. Green, you have even more books than my family!"

"I should've introduced Mom," Ben said.

"It's Ms., not Mrs., and O'Neill, not Green," said his mother.

"Susanna and I had a problem with mistaken identities when I first met her dad," Ben said, and I smiled, remembering.

"Benjamin says you've been tutoring him," his mother said.

"He's been doing fine on his own lately. He's sure to pass."

"Pass." Ms. O'Neill's expression became humorous as she quickly rolled her eyes, but her voice sounded sad as she repeated the word. "Pass."

"Be right back," Ben said, making a fast exit.

Turning, she watched him go. She turned to me, with a half-smile. "Oh, dear, I should have said how glad I am that you've helped Benjamin avoid the worst. I've certainly found it more pleasant to be with him lately, since he's wearing the swine's snout less often." Her half-smile became a whole.

I smiled back. "I agree with you about that."

Ben came in and bowed low. "Dinner is served," he said.

We went into the dining room — not the kitchen. I realized what the familiar aroma was when Ben took the top off a tureen and ladled out bowls of Jerry's vegetable soup.

"I called Jerry and got all the recipes from him," he said.

"My son's never so much as boiled water before," his mom said.

"You did a wonderful job, Ben. I feel honored," I said. "It must've taken you all day."

"That, and writing the last English composition," he said.

The essay had to be about Father's Day, but I didn't mention it. "Ben really is a good reader and writer," I told his mom.

"You're sweet to reassure me, Susanna, but I'm aware of Benjamin's abilities," she said. "I taught him to read when he was three years old, and I wrote down

121

the poems and stories he made up until he was five, and began doing it himself."

My spoonful of soup stopped outside my mouth.

"When Benjamin was ten, he typed out seventeen pages he titled 'A Child's Introduction to Greek Mythology.' "

I blinked.

"Benjamin, show Susanna your kindergarten photo."

He closed his eyes for a second. Then he got up, left the room, and minutes later returned with a framed photo of a small, bespectacled boy, with a solemn expression. He looked like an old man!

"I was sure he'd become a great scholar," his mother said.

I looked at Ben, who was deadpan . . . until he crossed his eyes.

"Long before he started school, Benjamin had a remarkable thirst for knowledge," his mother went on. "At five, he began to enjoy reading the encyclopedia so much that each night he fell asleep with at least one volume." She looked at Ben and sighed.

Bright red, Ben sighed, too, in a perfect imitation of hers. He said, "I was the inspiration for Little Lowell Look-It-Up."

"Excuse me?" I said.

"My mother's a writer," he said. "She wrote the Look-It-Up Family series."

"You're kidding," I said. But Ben shook his head. Softly, he said, "You were ready for Beaver Cleaver's mom, right?"

"I was ready for Yogi Berra." Amazed, I turned to his mother. "You're Kate O'Neill?"

"Yes."

I couldn't believe this. I just sat there, stunned.

"Susanna, are you all right?" Ben's mom asked, sounding half-amused and half-concerned.

"Mrs. Green . . . I mean, Ms. O'Neill . . . I . . . I love the Look-It-Up Family!"

"Thank you," she said with a smile.

But I hate you, Ben Green, I thought. I felt my face redden as I looked at his, which was also turning red. How could he keep this from me? It was a lie, a big lie. And I'd been thinking how close we'd been getting. I'd been thinking he was my friend.

"Susanna." Ben's voice was soft and kind of hoarse. As upset as I was, I could see that he was also upset. "I should've gotten the guts sooner," he said.

I remembered then that when he called to invite me to dinner, he said he'd been wanting to do it for a while, but didn't have the guts.

"I'm sorry it took so long, but I'm glad you're meeting Mom." There was so much feeling in Ben's voice and on his face!

I wanted to ask him a million questions, but I didn't want to be rude to his mom. I definitely didn't. In fact, I had a big question for her. "Ms. O'Neill, the latest Look-It-Up Family book came out a few years ago. Are you writing any more? I hope I hope I hope."

"Yes, but I'm a slow writer to begin with, and since my books aren't best-sellers I can't support Benjamin and myself by writing, so I also work as a freelance copy editor."

"What's that?"

"Publishing companies hire me to check the facts and the grammar of manuscript," she said. "I look up things for a living. Which is lucky, since Benjamin has hardly been a proper model for Little Lowell Look-

It-Up for several years." Her smile softened the sarcasm.

"Well . . ." I shrugged. "I guess nobody can be little forever."

"It's not physical changes that are the problem. It's his becoming an entirely different sort of person. The person sliding in the front door is not the person who read *Moby Dick* at age eleven."

He *had* read *Moby Dick*. I stared at Ben, who was bright red now. He was turning out to be very different from what I'd thought. Although not "entirely." So confusing! "I'm really glad to meet you," I told his mother. "I was glad to meet you as Ben's mom, but you're one of my favorite authors, and I never met a live one before."

"Only dead ones?" Ben said.

His mother laughed. She didn't seem to mind his being funny — if he was funny with words, not by wearing a pig's snout.

"Why haven't you told the whole town you're the famous Kate O'Neill?" I asked her.

She laughed again. "You'd be surprised how few people recognize any writer's name. And besides, I don't write so people will know my name. Writing's something I simply must do." She looked at Ben. "For the last few years, reading and writing have been things Benjamin has simply *not* wanted to do."

Ben said, "From the time I was around eleven, I've wanted to be a sports star. A funny guy, too. Nobody would suspect that a funny jock was a reader and writer. Not even his English teachers."

I looked down at the tablecloth, trying to sort all this out.

"Susanna, what's your very favorite book?" Ms. O'Neill asked me.

"*Wuthering Heights*," I said immediately.

"I adore it," she said.

"Me, too," said Ben.

With a smile, his mom said, "Only to you, Susanna, would Ben even admit he's read *Wuthering Heights*."

"My favorite's still *Moby Dick*, though," he said.

"What about your favorite, Ms. O'Neill?" I asked.

"Mmm . . . I'm torn between *War and Peace* and *Ramona the Pest*."

Ben and I had to laugh. "Susanna's doing something I'll bet you'd be interested in, Mom," Ben said. "She's gonna be the Library Story Lady, reading to kids and whoever else wants to come, starting Saturday."

"Susanna, that's lovely. Perhaps I'll come to hear you read."

"That'd be terrific," I said.

"I'll be there, too," Ben said.

His mom's face brightened at this. But it clouded as she said to me, "Your parents must be proud of you."

"Oh, sure. And they were also proud of me last year when I played the drums with Wild Women, an all-girl punk-rock band."

Ms. O'Neill looked at me, her eyes very bright, and kept looking. Finally, she said, "Susanna, you're a good friend to Benjamin."

"He's a good friend to me, too," I said.

"If you two will excuse me, I have some writing to do," she said. She stood up, gave me that firm handshake, then a full smile, and left.

"Whew, I feel like I've pitched a doubleheader," Ben said.

"I feel like I've pitched a tripleheader," I said.

"You know there's no such thing," Ben said.

"I don't know what I know," I said. "I thought I knew you."

Ben looked at me.

I'd enjoyed dinner with his mom, but now that he and I were alone together, I felt weird again about his lying to me for so long.

"Let's take a walk," he said.

"You can walk me home," I said, and my voice came out angry and hurt.

Outside, there were a million stars. We walked for a while in silence.

"I wish I'd told you sooner about my mom," Ben said, at last. "But if anybody knew my mom was a writer, they might suspect I wasn't just a funny jock."

I looked up at the stars.

"My mom's raised me by herself since my dad walked out," Ben said. "And by the way, he wasn't a rich businessman or a great athlete. He and my mom were grad students when he left. I don't know what he became."

"You and your mom haven't had *any* contact with him?"

"Nope."

That was so sad!

"For a long time, I thought he'd come back, or at least call or write me. Then when I got around eleven, it hit me that he wouldn't. That was also the time when the other guys were into sports, and everybody started calling me a nerd."

"It must've been awful," I said.

"I hated it." Ben kicked a stone into the gutter. "My mom kept wanting me to be Little Lowell Look-

It-Up. I wanted to be a *man.*" His voice shook when he said that last word.

We walked past our neighbors' houses. Once I would've thought I knew everything important about everybody inside. No more.

"It was good for me to quit reading and writing so much. Sports are great. And there're lots of important stuff you can't learn from books," Ben said. "But mostly I had to get away from my mom. She had such a tight grip on me for so long. It was just the two of us — reading and writing and looking things up together."

Ben was silent, and so was I. There were fireflies, little living lights, all around us.

"If her writing were going better, I bet she could really try to let me go, and let me find out for myself who I am. Maybe I did slow down her career when I wasn't Little Lowell anymore. . . ."

"Ben, you can't help that. You're not a character in a book."

"It sounds weird, Susanna, but sometimes I think my mom's more comfortable with literary characters than with real people. And when she creates her own characters, she can make them do whatever she wants, because they're part of her. But I'm not. I'm me."

"It sounds like you've thought this out."

"No joke. If I'd spent as much time studying English as I've spent trying to figure out my mom and me, I would've gotten an A +. I cooked dinner tonight to show her one of the things I've learned from your family — that I don't have to be the total opposite of Little Lowell, I don't have to be a joking jock, to be a man."

I didn't say a word, just smiled up at him.

"When I get home tonight, maybe my mom and I

can talk about it. I still want to do sports, I'll tell her, but I also want to get my grades up. It's not so easy to believe, though. Too bad school's almost over, so she won't see a decent report card until November. She'll be sighing all summer, which'll make me want to act gross."

"You'll think of a way to reassure your mom," I said. My voice was very strong as I added, "I just know it."

Silence. Then, very softly, Ben said, "Thanks for the vote of confidence, Susanna."

"You're welcome," I said, even more softly.

It was night, but not scary. The stars, the fireflies, and the streetlights were all shining. As Ben looked down at me, his blue eyes shone, too.

Nineteen

COME TO SATURDAY STORY HOUR! said the colorful poster on the library lawn. There were also signs in the schools and on the supermarket bulletin boards, and a notice in the newspaper.

"Maybe someday your name will be on the signs," Cassidy said.

"Susanna Siegelbaum Starring as the Saturday Story Lady," Ben teased me.

I laughed, but really was getting more excited every day. Mrs. Bannan and I chose the books. For the youngest kids, *The Little Engine That Could*. For the oldest, the first few chapters of *The Wind in the Willows*. For the "middle-aged kids," I suggested *The Look-It-Up Family*, and she enthusiastically agreed. I was tempted to say that Kate O'Neill was my friend Ben's mom, and she'd be coming to hear me. But I wasn't sure Ms. O'Neill would like that, so I kept quiet.

I practiced reading the books to Mrs. Bannan, and also to Cassidy, Ben, Sonya, Kelly, Amanda, and Elaine and Jerry. Finally, Cassidy said, "If I hear 'I think I can' once more, I think I'll be sick." Still, they all said I was a terrific reader and the kids would love the stories. Every compliment got me more geared up. The day before the first Story Hour, in fact, I had trouble concentrating on my everyday library work. Checking books in and out, I pictured myself in the center of the room, surrounded by a large, enraptured audience. "Wake up!" a kid yelled.

"No yelling in the library!" I yelled back.

Saturday morning I woke up wanting to shout, "I *know* I can!" I could almost hear the applause. Jerry and Elaine made me poachies — with ham, their comment on the acting I put into my reading.

Cassidy picked me up at nine. Her sisters would come to the library just before ten, when Story Hour was scheduled to start. It was already hot and humid. As Cassidy pushed her poker-straight hair behind her ears, I felt my curls tightening into corkscrews.

"What if everybody goes to the beach, and nobody comes to the library?" I said. "What if people come, but the heat makes them pass out? What if I pass out?"

"Everything will be wonderful," Cassidy said, but then she bit her lip.

"What's the matter?" I asked.

"My mother invited that man, what's-his-name, for dinner tonight."

"Eliot Henry's his name," I said. "No, wait — Henry Eliot."

"How *could* she?" said Cassidy, folding her arms. "I

130

don't want her to have a boyfriend. Not yet. I'm not ready."

"By the time you and the Stooges are all ready, your mom's boyfriend will have to pick her up at the Senior Citizens Center."

She looked down at her sneakered feet. "That's true."

We walked on. All around us, nature was lush, rich, gorgeous.

Still looking down at her sneakers, Cassidy spoke softly. "I still miss my father. I don't want my mother to replace him."

I almost said, "Don't be silly. Your mother doesn't want to replace your father." Instead, I bit my tongue.

"I know I'm being silly, but . . ." She uncrossed her arms, and twisted her fingers. "I miss Robby, too, but I've been too hurt and embarrassed to talk to him, much less try again to be friends with him."

"Oh," was all I said.

Turning to me, Cassidy squealed, "Siegelbaum, I'm jealous of my mother! I don't want her to have a boyfriend when I don't!" She giggled. "Doesn't that sound ridiculous?"

Smiling, I said, "Remember how jealous I was when you began going out with Robby?"

"Mm-hmm." She smiled a little, then shook her head. "But I still feel funny about meeting Henry Eliot. Will you come to dinner tonight? My mother knows I've been upset. She'll be glad to have you."

"I'd love to come." I'd bet anything Henry Eliot was really nice. Which reminded me of something. "Hey, Cassidy, when exactly is our bet up, anyway?"

"June twenty-first, which is . . . it's Monday! But we can make it midnight on Sunday."

"That's tomorrow! I can already taste that double-dip ice cream with sprinkles. Maybe mint chocolate chip and mocha fudge almond. Maybe . . ."

"Maybe you'll be dishing up ice cream for my sisters for the next year," Cassidy said. "You might still go out with a boy, or kiss one, or flirt with one. The boy of your dreams might show up at Story Hour."

"Yeah, sure," I said sarcastically.

"You never know."

I started to say, "I do so," but changed my mind.

We were at the library. The sun was so hot, and the humidity so high, I was tempted to take out my shoulder pads and use them as underarm shields.

Cassidy said, "Siegelbaum, I have a confession. I'm a little jealous that you're the Story Lady. I wish I were."

"Hey, thanks for telling me. That's a big compliment."

"You'll be wonderful," she said as we hugged.

Inside the library, it was cooler. Cassidy went to the adult and young adult section, and I went to the children's room. Mrs. Bannan greeted me at the door. "Are you nervous, dear?"

"Nah." Suddenly my stomach felt like a glass of Alka-Seltzer looked, my mouth felt like the Sahara, and my legs like rubber. "Maybe a teensy bit. But I'll be fine."

Someone tugged at my sweater. "Susanna, Susanna." It was Joey. "Read me a story?"

What a thrill — Joey was really interested in books! I'd tell Ben how influential he'd been. Too bad right now I had to concentrate on not fainting. "Please don't pull at me, Joey. And, no, I can't read you a story." I flashed a celebrity smile. "I'm the Story Lady."

"That's stupid. The Story Lady *oughta* read me a

story." Joey's lower lip came out, and he walked away. I wanted to go after him and explain, but was using all my energy staying conscious.

It was quarter to ten, and only a few regulars besides Joey were there. What if nobody else came? Ten was pretty early in the morning. Maybe this should've been scheduled for later.

As I looked at the clock for the twentieth time, some more regulars came in, smiling shyly at me. Arm in arm, Sonya and Kelly came in. Then, several kids and parents I didn't know. A minute later, Amanda bopped in. Cassidy's sisters ran in, Cassidy chasing after them. Elaine and Jerry walked in, smiling, and sat in the middle row of chairs. Ben and his mother came in, waved, and sat near the front. Did I have time to introduce Ms. O'Neill to my parents and friends? While wondering, I noticed that Amanda had somehow managed to sit between Sonya and Kelly. Lots more kids I didn't know came in. Then came a woman holding a notebook and pen, and a man holding a camera — the media!

When the reporter and photographer came my way, I suddenly stopped being scared and started being super-excited. Quickly sticking out my hand, I loudly announced, "Hi! I'm Susanna Siegelbaum, the Story Lady."

After we shook hands, and they introduced themselves, Mrs. Bannan said quietly, "And I'm Elinor Bannan, the librarian."

"Would you tell me a little about your background?" asked the reporter, her pen poised.

"How about a few photos?" the photographer said.

I stood very straight and smiled, trying to look both beautiful and brilliant. "I was born right here in town,"

I said. "I go to The Willow School. I've always loved to read. I . . ."

"Excuse me," said the reporter. "I was talking to Mrs. Bannan. Isn't she in charge here?"

"Could you let me get a photo of the librarian?" said the photographer, motioning me to get out of the way.

"Absolutely!" My smile stretched across my burning face, making me feel like a big red balloon . . . that any second could burst. I walked quickly to the ladies' room and leaned against the door.

What a show-off! What was this — Story Hour, or The Susanna Siegelbaum Show? My theme song should be one note and one word — me me me me me!

At the sink, I splashed cold water on my face and dried it with a paper towel. Looking in the mirror, I thought: If the reporter *had* asked my background, I could've said, "My friend Ben said it once — I keep trying to be the center of attention, know the answers, and make the rules."

But Ben later said that wasn't *always* true. And I also thought I'd changed. I'd been trying so hard.

Turning from my reflection, I walked over to the window. A crummy day. Still, I loved spring. Summer, too.

Cassidy'd been jealous of both her mom and me. Ben had admitted that he, too, liked the spotlight. Even Betty had been jealous of Bubby. I'd just have to keep trying to be a mensch.

There was a knock on the door. "Susanna?" It was Mrs. Bannan's voice. "Are you all right, dear? Everyone is looking forward to hearing you read."

How nice of her to reassure me. I'd never noticed before how pretty her voice was.

Her pretty voice gave me an idea.

Twenty

I opened the door and came out. Calmly and quietly, I said, "Mrs. Bannan, you have such a lovely voice. Are you sure you wouldn't like to be Story Lady, at least some of the time?"

"Thank you for the compliment," she said, with a sweet smile, "but it's not for me." Her brow furrowed. "You're not nervous, are you, dear?"

"Nope. I can hardly wait to start. It's just that . . . well, I know some other people who could do an excellent job as Story Lady. Story Hour was your idea, Mrs. Bannan. What would you think of having more than one reader?"

"I think it's a marvelous idea," she said. "And a generous one."

This time when I reddened, it wasn't from shame. "My friend Annie Cassidy could read *The Little Engine*

That Could. She's had lots of practice reading to her little sisters."

"Of course. Annie's always been a wonderful reader."

"And my friend Ben Green would do a great job with *The Look-It-Up Family.*"

"I think it's important for the children, especially the boys, to see a male reading." Mrs. Bannan looked at the clock. "But Story Hour must start in just a few minutes, Susanna."

"It will," I said. I caught Cassidy's eye, and then Ben's, and beckoned them to a corner of the room.

"What's up?" Ben asked, while Cassidy was saying, "Is something wrong, Siegelbaum?"

"Mrs. Bannan and I were thinking it would be fun to have several Story Ladies. . . ." I looked at Ben. "I mean, Story Persons. We were wondering if you two would like to read today."

Cassidy turned white, and Ben red. But how quickly Cassidy recovered! "I'd like it a lot," she said, and we hugged.

"Ben, it's really and truly okay if you say no," I told him.

He glanced over at his mother.

"Maybe you'd like to read *The Wind in the Willows* instead of your mom's book? Or maybe you'd like to read a whole other book another Saturday?"

No answer. I looked at the clock. Still no answer. I looked at Mrs. Bannan, who was looking at me.

"I'll do it," Ben said. Only he didn't look too thrilled about it.

"You sure?"

"I'm sure." He even smiled a little.

Grinning, I nodded at Mrs. Bannan, who then

walked to the lectern, facing the audience. "Welcome, everyone," she said. "Thank you so much for coming to the first Saturday Story Hour. I'm pleased to tell you that our Story Lady, Susanna Siegelbaum, has asked two of her friends to join her in reading to you today. So we will hear a variety of voices from these several Story . . ."

If she said Story Ladies, what would Ben do? Act goofy? Leave? Should I yell out "Story Persons"?

"From these several Storytellers," Mrs. Bannan continued smoothly. "First, Annie Cassidy will read *The Little Engine That Could.*"

I led the applause while Cassidy walked over to the lectern, where Mrs. Bannan had placed the book. Cassidy opened the book, and began to read in a whisper.

"Turn it up!" yelled a kid. It was Chrissy.

It took a few more sentences, but Cassidy's voice got stronger. She'd read that book so many times — first to herself, then to her sisters — she practically knew it by heart. Reading "I think I can, I think I can, I think I can," her shyness completely disappeared! Was she realizing how much she'd changed, how much braver she'd become? She'd gone out with Robby, stood up to me, was going to try out for her school's literary magazine. Now she was taking center stage — and enjoying it.

The applause was, as reviewers sometimes write, "tumultuous." The Stooges yelled, "Hooray!"

"And now, Benjamin Green will read *The Look-It-Up Family,*" said Mrs. Bannan.

Would Ben have an arrow going through his head? He didn't, but obviously wished he did. When he faced the audience, I saw his eyes start to cross. Then Joey gave him the V for victory. Grinning, Ben gave Joey one back — and began to bellow. Wow, was he loud. Almost clownish. But at the end of the first page, when he got to his first big laugh, he settled down. He read amazingly well. He was funny, smart, and warm. Little Lowell Look-It-Up had always been laughable and likeable, but Ben made him lovable.

Afterward there was loud applause, and Ben's mom held a tissue to her eyes.

"Thanks a lot," Ben said. "This wasn't planned, but . . . I want to introduce the author of the book — my mom, Kate O'Neill." Everyone turned, applauding even louder, as she half-stood, smiling. The reporter headed toward her, but she shook her head, put her finger to her lips, and then pointed toward the front.

"Our last story today will be read by the young woman who was the inspiration for Saturday Story Hour, through her reading to the children as a volunteer here at the library," said Mrs. Bannan. "I hope Susanna Siegelbaum will inspire more people, young and old, to help out in our community in whichever way they wish. And I hope all our Storytellers will bring more and more people to the library."

There was applause.

I went to the lectern, kind of glowing from Mrs. Bannan's words. I held up *The Wind in the Willows*, showing the cover. "The books are the real stars here," I said.

When I began to read, I was surprised that my mouth felt dry, and my voice was kind of quavery. It took me a couple of pages to get into the story. But soon I felt what I always felt when I read — excited and comforted at the same time.

As I read on, I found I knew the story so well that I could look up often at the people in the audience.

I could tell by the expressions on their faces that they were as enchanted as I. It made me feel close to them all.

All at once, I could feel the love that went into all the times my parents read to me, my teachers read to me, and Cassidy and I read to each other. I thought how great it was that Ben and I could talk about sports *and* books. Saying the words that ended the chapter, I felt as if the characters in the book, the person who wrote the book, the people in the audience, and I myself, were all one big family. What a feeling!

"More! More!" somebody shouted as people applauded.

"Kenneth Grahame's *The Wind in the Willows* will be continued next week," I said.

Then Mrs. Bannan was next to me, and Cassidy and Ben, and Amanda, Kelly, and Sonya, and Joey, and Chrissy, Lisa, and Jane. We all started hugging one another.

"You were fantastic," I told Cassidy.

"Siegelbaum, so were you. And it was so nice of you to remember that I wanted to be Story Lady."

"Even the Stooges looked like they were enjoying it," I said.

"They really were," Cassidy said. She looked around. "But where are they?" I pointed at them as they raced toward the door. "I'll call you," said Cassidy, dashing after them.

"Considering that this wasn't a rock concert, it wasn't too bad," Amanda said.

"Thanks a lot," I said, laughing.

Sonya said, "Kelly and I have been talking to Amanda. We told her how we both play guitar, and we found out she sings — real soul stuff."

Kelly said, "So, Susanna, how'd you like to play the drums with the rock group we're thinking of putting together?"

"Why not?" I said. We made a date to talk about it, and Sonya, Amanda, and Kelly left together, talking excitedly.

Then Ben was holding out his hand, and I was shaking it. "You were terrific," I said.

"You, too." He grinned.

"Your mom looked so proud of you."

"Yeah."

"And afterward, Ben, you showed her how proud *you* were of *her*."

"Yeah."

"Hey, what's going on? Now that some people know you can read really well, are you feeling so weird about it that you'll only speak in one-syllable words?"

"Amyotrophic lateral sclerosis," he said.

"Huh?"

"That's the big, long Latin term for Lou Gehrig's disease. I wanted to tell you that time you were talking to Jerry and me about it, but I still needed to be macho then. And, anyway, you totally took over."

Just then Joey came up and yanked on Ben's shirt. "Will you read me a story, Story Lady?"

"Jeez, I've gone far from macho fast," Ben said.

Joey said, "Ben, when I'm a big guy like you, I want to be a Story Lady, too."

Ben and I cracked up. "I'll read you one story," Ben said. "Then I'm gonna play ball." Joey slipped his hand in Ben's as they walked toward the bookshelves. "But maybe I'll stop by the library next week and read some more," Ben said. "And maybe I'll show you how to turn a piece of paper into a dinosaur."

Elaine and Jerry emerged from the bunch of parents and kids around Mrs. Bannan and Ms. O'Neill. "Weren't Cassidy and Ben great?" I said.

"They certainly were," Elaine said. "And we introduced ourselves to Ben's mother. What a wonderful coincidence that she's the author of some of your favorite books."

"I love how he pointed her out. He's really proud of her."

"We're proud of *you*," Jerry said, putting his arm around me.

"We're coming to hear you again next week," said Elaine.

"I bet you'll hear Cassidy and Ben again, too," I said. "And maybe some other readers."

"We'd like that," said Jerry. "But now, after all that reading, how about a little something to soothe your throat?"

I was wondering whether he meant cough drops, when he continued. "Say an ice-cream soda?"

Mmm mm mmm, was that good.

Twenty-one

"Do you really think Henry Eliot will still be interested in my mother after he meets my sisters?" Cassidy greeted me when I arrived at her house for dinner that evening.

Jane was pretending to slice a loaf of bread the way black belts in karate split wood — with the heel of her hand. Lisa was crying because one of the pink satin ribbons streaming from her hair had fallen into the gravy. Chrissy was announcing that because of her love for animals, she was now a vegetarian, and would rather starve than eat the main course. As Cassidy put the roast leg of lamb on a platter, Chrissy bleated, "Baaaaaa!"

"He's from New England, where people are very proper," Cassidy said. "And he's a bachelor, so he's probably not even used to one *normal* kid."

"Wow, wait'll he meets the Stooges."

The doorbell rang, and Cassidy almost dropped the roast.

"I'll get it," I said, running through the living room and whipping open the front door.

A tall, thin man with sandy hair, deep brown eyes, and a nice, big nose smiled down at me. "Hello, I'm Henry Eliot. You must be . . ." He laughed. "Which one *are* you?"

"I'm Susanna Siegelbaum, Annie's friend."

"Hello, Susanna." His smile got broader as he looked toward the stairs. "Maggie, you look beautiful."

Maggie? I turned around. Oh, Margaret . . . Mrs. Cassidy! She smiled at me. "I knew I could count on Susanna not to be shy."

Grinning, I scooted out of the way.

"Henry, I'd like you to meet my daughters. Girls . . . ?"

The Cassidy kids came into the room and shook Henry Eliot's hand. Chrissy giggled, Lisa curtsied, Jane grunted, and Cassidy looked as if she might cry.

We sat down in the dining room to eat. As Mrs. Cassidy began to serve, the rest of us stared at Henry Eliot. "Call me Henry," he said. Silence.

"What interesting things have been going on that you girls would like to tell Henry?" Mrs. Cassidy said.

"We buried Lulu," Chrissy said.

"Yeah, Lulu croaked," Jane said. "T.T. croaked, too."

"Lulu's funeral was extremely beautiful," said Lisa. "Especially Ben's sermon, about how Lulu was small and slimy."

"Oh?" Henry said.

"You might tell Henry that these aren't people you girls are talking about — they're pets," Mrs. Cassidy said.

"Ah," said Henry.

"Let's tell Henry about Harvey," Chrissy said.

"Harvey who?" I asked.

"Harvey the hamster," Chrissy replied, pulling Harvey from her shirt pocket. Harvey jumped out of her hand and ran under the table.

"Help!" Lisa leaped up, screeching.

"Key-iiiiiii!" Jane jumped up, bent down, and tried to halve Harvey with a karate chop.

Chrissy got up and then disappeared under the table. Seconds later she came back, kissing Harvey.

"Yuch, the urge!" Jane yelled. The three girls chanted: "The urge, the urge, the urge to regurge./ The urge to regurgitate, and throw up all the food you ate./V-O-M-I-T, vomit!" They put their fingers down their throats and gagged.

Mrs. Cassidy closed her eyes. Henry was blinking fast. Cassidy rolled her eyes, and in reply, I crossed mine.

At last, Henry spoke. Looking down at his plate, he calmly said, "This looks like a supah suppah."

The girls giggled. "Hey, say that again," Jane said.

"What? 'Supah suppah'?"

More giggles. "Mom, he talks funny," Chrissy said.

"Me? Talk funny?" Henry said. "It cahn't be. Bostonians don't talk funny. I had no idear . . ."

All the Stooges sat down, laughing and laughing. Mrs. Cassidy said, "Girls, please stop that."

"I cahn't," Jane said.

"I have no idear how to," said Lisa.

"Besides, I think it's supah," said Chrissy.

"Jane, how would you like to spah with me?" Henry asked.

"Spah? Is that a place with gurgling water?" Jane asked.

I translated from the Bostonian. "Henry means spar."

"You mean fight, like in karate?" Jane said to Henry. "You know karate?"

After swallowing a mouthful of food, he said, "Some."

"Got any belts?"

Henry dabbed at his mouth with his napkin. "Black." Passing the gravy boat to Jane, he said, "Care for more?"

Jane took the gravy, without taking her eyes off Henry.

"I'm interested in your pets' funerals, Chrissy," Henry went on. "Some people find it morbid to talk about such things, but most New Englanders don't. In Boston there are many old graveyards that are fascinating as history and art. People make rubbings of the gravestones."

"I learned how in art class," Lisa said. "You put a cloth on the gravestone, rub with a special pencil, and the markings show."

"That's the idear," Henry said.

The girls laughed, and he smiled.

"I'm changing Harvey's name to Henry," Chrissy announced.

"Chrissy, I'm honored," said Henry.

The rest of the evening was really fun. Everybody got into the conversation. Even — finally — Cassidy. It turned out that Henry liked *Pride and Prejudice*, Cassidy's all-time favorite book. Not only that, his

Aunt Hetty was a member of The Jane Austen Society, a kind of fan club for the book's author, who Cassidy practically idolized.

When I left, Cassidy came on the porch with me. "He's nice, isn't he?" she said.

"Yup," I said.

"It's not his accent or his black belt or what he knows about gravestones that makes me like him, though. It's not even the Jane Austen part," she said.

"What is it?"

"Look at Mom." When we peeked in, Mrs. Cassidy was glowing.

"I'm so happy for her," Cassidy said. Then: "Siegelbaum, do you think I should call Robby and ask if we can get together, not steadily, but sometimes?"

"I don't know," I said. "What do *you* think?"

"Siegelbaum, you've actually changed!"

I didn't deny it.

"You and Ben are good friends now," Cassidy said.

"Uh-huh. Who would've believed it?"

"Are you sure you're not more than friends?"

Was she crazy? "Sure I'm sure."

"Really? Are you absolutely positively certain?"

I glared at her. Who could be absolutely positively certain of anything?

Looking at her watch, she said, "If you don't flirt with a boy, date a boy, or kiss a boy in the next twenty-four hours, you'll win our bet."

"Call me at one second after midnight tomorrow. To congratulate me."

Cassidy laughed. "Don't be so sure *you* won't be congratulating *me*."

Twenty-two

I smiled all day Sunday. Playing drums with Ringo Starr, sunbathing with Elaine, cooking with Jerry, talking on the phone with Bubby, I smiled. Ben and his mom were coming to dinner!

They arrived at seven, and at ten we were still talking, laughing, and eating.

"Here, Ben, have my Tofutti. I'm full." I passed him my frozen-tofu dessert. Elaine and Jerry exchanged glances. Nice of them not to announce this was the first time in my life I'd given away my dessert!

"If I were starting a Tofutti business," Ms. O'Neill said, "my first flavor would be tutti-frutti-Tofutti."

"You could advertise it with a rock song that Susanna's group could play," Ben said. "It could start, 'Tutti-frutti-Tofutti, all-a-rootie.' "

"You two are so good with words," Elaine said.

"So good," Jerry said, "that we Siegelbaums will give

147

you the ultimate compliment of challenging you to a game of Scrabble."

An hour and forty-five minutes later, Elaine was saying, "Jerry, you can't make 'impress' into 'Impressionism.' The art movement starts with a capital I."

"Give me a break, Elaine. You use medical terms. Who else would make 'urge' into 'surgery'?"

"Try playing with Cassidy and her parochial-school words," I said. "She once made 'fix' into 'crucifix.' And Bubby uses words like 'shlemiel' and 'shlemazel,' which aren't even English; they're Yiddish."

"Look at the grin on Ben's face. He probably thinks he's going to win," Jerry said.

"Nope. I'm just having fun," Ben said.

"Marvelous," said his mother, "because *I'm* about to win." Around my measly "lo," she put all seven of her letters, including an "x" and "y," making "xylophone."

Elaine, Jerry, Ben, and I groaned. "This calls for a rematch," Elaine said.

"Soon," said Ms. O'Neill, as she stood up. "It was a lovely evening. Thanks so much for having Benjamin and me. It's almost midnight. . . ."

I looked at the clock: ten of.

"I'll help Susanna clear the table and be home right after, Mom," Ben said.

Ms. O'Neill said good-night to Elaine, Jerry, and me, then the three adults went to the front door together. Elaine and Jerry came back and said good-night to Ben and me. As Jerry turned to go, Ben very lightly punched him in the shoulder. He and Jerry smiled at each other. Then, hand in hand, Jerry and Elaine left for their room.

"Susanna, there's something I want you to read,"

Ben said. From his back pocket, he pulled out a folded piece of paper, handing it to me.

After unfolding the paper, I scanned it. "This is an essay — the Father's Day essay we had to write for English class."

He just nodded.

To myself, I read: " 'My Father, by Ben Green . . . I don't know my father. He disappeared when I was a baby. As long as I can remember, my mother, Kate O'Neill, has been both a mother and a father to me. When I first got this assignment, I considered making up a father — a rich, famous, and powerful man like a corporation president, a military hero, or a sports star. Next, I considered writing about my mother, but I already did that in my Mother's Day essay. So, I decided to write about a man I know. His name is Jerry Siegelbaum.' "

I swallowed, and went on. " 'My mother has shown me that a woman can be the breadwinner in a family, a woman can be hardworking and strong, and can inspire her child to achieve and to have great ambitions. These are important lessons. Recently, though, through Jerry Siegelbaum, I have learned other, equally important lessons.' "

Reading on, I began to smile. " 'Jerry Siegelbaum has shown me that a man can be the breadmaker in the family, a man can be gentle and kind, and can inspire others to appreciate and enjoy, as well as to achieve. So, on Father's Day, I would like to honor my mother, for being both mother and father to me, and I would like to express my appreciation for the enjoyment brought into my life by Jerry Siegelbaum . . . my friend.' "

I just looked at the paper for a minute. Then I looked

149

at Ben. "This is beautiful. You should be a writer. Oops, forget I said that. You should be whatever you want to be."

As Ben laughed, I spotted a Scrabble letter under the table, bent down to pick it up, and getting up again, hit my head.

"Ow!" I plopped to the floor, holding my head.

"Susanna, did you hurt yourself?" Ben rushed to kneel next to me.

"No, no, I'm fine," I moaned.

"Are you sure?" He looked very concerned.

"I'm sure," I said, smiling.

Ben smiled back, and then there was a silence. "Susanna, usually when it's quiet, one of us says something funny," he said.

"Lately I've been trying to be dull," I said.

"Don't overdo it," he said. But we didn't laugh. Instead, we looked at each other. "Susanna . . ." Ben's face reddened. "I really like you."

Feeling warm all over, I said, "I like you, too."

"I like you more than I like Dizzy, Dazzy, and Daffy," he said.

"Daffy Dean or Daffy Duck?"

"Both."

"Wow. Well, I like you more than I like Bronko Nagurski, Bulldog Turner, Bruiser Kinard, and Branwell Brontë — put together," I said.

"I like you more than No-Neck Williams, Cukoo Christensen, Pretzels Pezzullo, and Goober Zuber," he said.

Laughing, I said, "Three months ago, before I met you and learned about baseball, I would've thought you made up those names."

"Three months ago, before I got to know you, I sat next to you with a button on my toga," Ben said. "Remember what it said?"

That seemed so long ago! I had to think for a few seconds. "Oscula me . . . ?"

"Thought you'd never ask," Ben said, tilting his head a little as he leaned toward me.

I tilted and leaned, too. I closed my eyes. Gently, so gently, we kissed.

The clock struck midnight. A second later, the phone rang, and a second after that, Elaine and Jerry came into the room.

"Excuse us," Elaine said, looking down on the floor as Ben and I drew away from each other and turned many shades of red. "I forgot my glasses," Jerry said.

Ben and I scrambled up. I ran to the phone, grabbed it, and said, "Hi, Cassidy. Call you back in a minute," then hung up.

"Elaine, Jerry, there's something I forgot to tell you," I said. "Ben hasn't really been my boyfriend."

Elaine nodded, while Jerry said, "Oh." Neither looked fazed.

"Let me explain," I said. "I got Ben to pretend to be my boyfriend, so you'd be happy I was seeing a boy, but I could still win my bet with Cassidy that I could give up boys for three months . . . which I just lost."

"Will you explain that again in the morning?" Elaine asked.

"We have faith in you, Susanna. We know everything'll be fine," Jerry said, and they left.

Ben started to laugh. "Just one minute, okay?" I said. As he nodded, I dialed the phone. "Congratulations, Cassidy."

"Siegelbaum, you mean you dated, flirted with, or kissed a boy? You kissed Ben, didn't you? I just know you kissed Ben."

"You got it."

"Oh, Siegelbaum, I was sure it would happen. I was absolutely positively certain you two liked each other as more than friends."

"Cassidy, you sound just like me. You . . ."

"I called Robby and asked him out," she interrupted. "He said yes. I'll tell you all about it tomorrow." She paused. "Are you very upset about losing the bet?"

I thought about it. "Nope. It's been an interesting three months. I've learned a lot, and had lots of fun."

"Maybe you'll learn and have fun baby-sitting with my sisters."

That, I didn't want to think about. "Good-night, Cassidy."

"Good-night, Siegelbaum."

Ben said, "Susanna, what's the story? Now you have to baby-sit with Jane, Lisa, and Chrissy?"

"And Harvey the hamster," I said. "No, make that Henry the hamster." I crossed my eyes.

When I uncrossed them, Ben's eyes were very bright, and he was smiling. "I'll help you," he said.

"Hey, thanks."

I, Susanna Siegelbaum, had to give up guys to find a boyfriend who was also a friend.

It was worth it.